# HERE THERE BE MONSTERS

## SPACE ROGUES

### BOOK 8

## JOHN WILKER

EDITED BY

CHRISTINA SHORT

Rogue Publishing

# CONTENTS_

**Space Rogues Universe (in story chronological order)**

- Space Rogues 1: The Epic Adventures of Wil Calder, Space Smuggler
- Space Rogues 2: Big Ship, Lots of Guns
- Space Rogues 3: The Behemoth Job
- Space Rogues 4: Stay Warm, Don't Die
- Space Rogues 5: So This is Earth?
- Space Rogues 6: War and Peace
- Space Rogues 7: A Guy Walks Into a Bar
- Space Rogues 8: Here, There Be Monsters

## CHARACTERS_

Our Heros

- Wil Calder
- Cynthia Luar
- Zephyr
- Maxim
- Bennie
- Gabe

Other People We Meet

- Barbara Mress: Tygran female. CEO of Tralgot Corporation. Assigned to manage the dismantling of Farsight Corporation assets and programs by the GC Governing council.
- Councilwoman Selmak: Member of the GC Governing Council.
- Jacoby - Multonae male - Bigger than Maxim. Like a giant roach with a semi human face. No eyes.

- Sekma - Sylban male - Eyeless. 4 inch thorns sprout from his body. unable to speak.
- Breeze - Palorian female - Elongated head. Arms twice as long as normal, long thin fingers. Hairless. Arms extend fleshy membranes turning into bar wings. Can alter light around her to become invisible.
- Folit - Trollack male - Arms turned into clumps of tentacles. No legs. Torso ends in stump.
- Bol Kar - malkorite male - Looks like a spider. Can spin webs that are stronger than most manufactured cable. Has no teeth and can only digest liquified food.
- Wlen - Brailack female - Head covered in fleshy dreadlocks. No eyes. Mouth extended to width of head. Can change mass to grow or shrink. Has large pouch under mouth like a bullfrog.
- Demfley - Olop female -Looks like a sea turtle/llama hybrid. Hands that are flippers. Hairy but with chunks of black chitin underneath. Hair comes out under the armor scales. Can hardly move around on her own. Can only maneuver in space as long as her tank is full.
- T'Kinlo - Trenbal female - Tail grew spikes, scales grew into larger chitinous pieces. Constant pain as scales continue to grow until falling out. Fleshy tentacles grow out from under the scales.
- Nellin: Tygran male. Leader of Shadow Six, the GC's secret off-the-books special ops team.
- Toph: Olop female. Member of Shadow Six
- Branx: Malkorite male. Member of Shadow Six
- Len: Research droid. Currently residing on Arcadia

# PART ONE

# CHAPTER 1_

# THE INTERGALACTIC DREAM OF
HOME OWNERSHIP_

"And as you can see, this level is mostly bare walls, perfect for—"
The broker looks at Wil again. "What did you say you all did again?"

"Import export." Wil smiles. "Vandalay Industries is an importer
exporter."

"Of what?" the crystalline being says, her voice coming from a
metal box affixed to her body, like someone speaking over wind
chimes.

Wil wiggles a hand. "Oh, you know...this and that." He looks
around. "Anyway, good to know we can build this floor out as needed.
You said you had some contractors you trust?"

A thin mechanical arm raises to touch an icon on her PADD.
"Oh yes, I'll forward them to you." Wil nods.

They're in a warehouse on the outskirts of Fury, only a half kilometer from the main spaceport, and more importantly, at least to Wil,
less than a twenty-minute walk to a bar. Not a bar Wil is familiar
with, but walkability beats familiarity.

As they head up the stairs to the third level, Cynthia asks, "And
the supports are rated for what we need?"

The broker, a single meter-long piece of crystal in a metal support
frame that provides her arms and legs, says, "Oh, yes. The ground

floor mechanical bay supports are twice the regulation thickness. The previous tenants kept the second floor full of cargo modules. Quite heavy. Hence, the reinforcements."

"Why did they leave?" Maxim asks as they reach the third and final floor. A wide hallway bisects this floor. Along either side of the hallway are bedrooms and what the broker described earlier as a vault. Matching stairwells anchor each end of the hallway, with a lift that at the moment isn't functional, in the northeast corner of the building.

"They were raided by Peacekeepers," the broker replies as she enters a spacious bedroom with floor-to-ceiling windows. "Apparently, they were slavers who specialized in Ruknak."

Ignoring the disturbing revelation, Wil says, "Dibs. This one is Cyn's and mine." Zephyr sighs. Wil looks at her. "What? Oh, the slaver thing. That's horrible. If this place can hold a few hundred Ruknak on each floor, we should be good," he adds.

When Cynthia pinches his midsection, he looks over at her. "What? I didn't say I supported slaving. I don't, but a Ruknak is as good a unit of measure as any." He walks to the windows. "And this view ain't bad."

"Explains the price," Maxim adds. When Zephyr gives him a look, he adds, "What? No one wants a warehouse that used to be full of slaves." He looks past Wil, out the window. "I suppose the views on Fury don't get any better." Beyond the window is the spaceport, and off to the side, the night market. A blocky freighter is lumbering up and out of the port, its engines roaring. "Good soundproofing," Maxim adds.

"Except us," Wil deadpans, turning to look at the others. Zephyr and Cynthia both sigh, sharing an apologetic look with the crystalline being showing them around for the second time. They look at the other bedrooms, agreeing that the smaller room, farther from the rest, will be Bennie's.

They return to the ground floor via the second stairwell. The ground floor sports a ten-meter-high ceiling, more than enough room for the *Ghost*. Bennie and Gabe, currently on Arcadia, have already signed off on the building and its infrastructure. Gabe is especially pleased with the hangar space and the sizable mechanic's bay in the back.

"So, can I tell the owner you'll take it?"

Wil looks around, making a show of slowly spinning to take the entire hangar space in, humming as he does. "Yeah, we'll take it." He holds up a finger. "With a ten percent discount. The slaving thing wasn't disclosed." He smiles.

The broker makes a noise like glass shards being ground together. She backs away. "I will see what the owner says." She moves toward the open main doors of the space. The dusty brown of Fury and its mostly uniform brown block buildings lie beyond.

Zephyr says, "I do like it. We still clear with space control but avoid spaceport fees."

Wil nods, putting an arm around Cynthia's waist. "The purchase plus renovations will wipe out a good chunk of our reserves, but that whole skimming thing we set up with ol' What's His Face is delivering nicely."

"Bonson Drell," Zephyr offers. Wil ignores her.

The broker walks back, her metallic feet clicking on the duracrete floor. "We have a deal!" she exclaims, holding her PADD up as she approaches.

# RENOVATIONS_



"You sure they're trustworthy?" Cynthia asks after Wil ends a call with the contractor he chose from the broker's list. They're sitting at the kitchen table on the *Ghost,* now parked in the spacious hangar of the warehouse. The deal closed that morning and the team wastes no time in relocating.

Wil shrugs. "Hell if I know. Her list was lengthy, and these are the ones who outfitted Bennie's workshop, so I assume they're at least okay."

From the sofa, Maxim says, "Given that this is Fury, that's about the best I'd hope for."

"Right?" Zephyr agrees. She chuckles. "It was genuinely a pleasure to see the look on Jussip's stinky smug face when I told him we would no longer be renting space in the port."

Wil grins. "Wish I could have seen it."

"When can they start?" Maxim asks.

"Next week, which is nice. We've got that job to get to, and then we have to pick up Gabe and his royal green asshole-ness on Arcadia. Then we can pop in and see how they're doing."

"Oh, right, hauling livestock," Maxim grumbles.

Wil points a finger. "Hey, I gave you the option to find something better. All you came up with was that gig helping overthrow a government."

Maxim tuts. "I still don't understand the problem. That sounded really fun."

"Love, it's a legitimate, elected government," Zephyr says.

Maxim shrugs. "Not ours."

Wil watches his friends for a bit, then says, "Okay, well, we leave tomorrow morning, so I'm thinking we order in and watch the new *Star Crusader* flick I got from James."

Cynthia groans. "The last one was so cheesy."

Zephyr nods. "Yeah, even by Earth entertainment standards."

Wil puts his hands on his chest. "You all wound me." After a beat, he says, "So...Lupnil's or Mama Golka's?"

"Lupnil's," everyone in the lounge says.

Zephyr smiles. "Since Bennie isn't here, we don't have to worry about the gas."

Maxim shudders. "It's like he's rotting inside."

Zephyr reaches for a PADD sitting on the arm of the sofa and taps on it for a minute or two, then looks up. "Food's on its way." She sets the PADD down. "This is a big step for us, you know?"

Wil looks over. "I mean, I always assumed we'd be *Golden Girl*ing it. We're just one step closer now." He grins. "Picture it, Fury..."

Maxim looks at Zephyr, then Cynthia. "*Golden Girl*ing? I am not planning on changing my gender."

She raises an eyebrow. "Or color?" He nods.

Wil smiles. "*Golden Girls* now added to the Educate the Aliens About Earth queue."

Cynthia looks at the two Palorians. "We're probably going to regret this."

Maxim nods. "Indeed." He inclines his head toward Zephyr. "She's not wrong, though. This is big, a physical base of operations. An address that keeps us in one place."

Wil shrugs. "Yeah, but it's not like we don't use Fury as our base of operations already. We just do it from the *Ghost* on a random spaceport pad. Now we have a place we send potential clients to and receive space junk mail."

# LIKE A WESTERN_

As THE *GHOST* leaves the atmosphere of Fury, Zephyr looks over to Wil. "I officially vote that we never watch another *Star Crusader* movie. That franchise can't die fast enough. I'd rather watch Brailack thrillers."

Before Wil can protest, Cynthia says, "Seconded."

He looks over his shoulder as the main display changes from wispy clouds to pitch black and stars. "Et tu, Brute?"

Cynthia stares at him. "Whatever that means, yes."

Wil sighs. "I'll admit, it was bad. I don't know why they keep giving that guy directorial work. It's like all he knows how to do is blow things up and over saturate shots with lens flare."

They pass a few large freighters slogging their way up and out of Fury's gravity well. A light on Wil's console comes to life. He pushes the FTL throttle forward. The pinpoints of light on the main display stretch into rainbow lines as the *Ghost* leaps into faster-than-light travel.

Wil turns. "Two days to the pickup. Who's making lunch?"

"You have to make sure they eat," the gangly, red-skinned man says two days later. All four arms are resting on his hips as he watches Maxim and Zephyr guide the loud creatures up the cargo ramp. He turns back to Wil. "They don't much care for space travel, so won't be wanting to eat, but you gotta make 'em."

Wil looks at the creatures. "How, exactly?" The large, segmented creatures are shuffling their many feet. While low to ground, the creatures are as bulky as cows.

The alien rancher shrugs his uppermost set of shoulders. "Oh, it's not that hard. You just gotta hold the kibbles in front of 'em for a bit. They'll get it."

Wil grimaces. "Great."

From the cargo hold, Maxim shouts, "They're all in."

Wil turns to the man. "Anything else?"

The man shakes his head. "Nope, that's it. Keep 'em fed, they'll be fine."

Wil mimes touching the brim of a cowboy hat. "Sounds good, pardner. We're off."

The multi-limbed man raises an eyebrow ridge. "We are not business partners. This is a one-time arrangement."

Wil waves his hand. "It's an expression."

"A confusing one," the other man whispers as he turns and walks away from the *Ghost*.

As Wil enters the cargo bay, he slaps his palm on the control pedestal just inside the large cargo doors. As the cargo doors grind closed, he pushes the rump of one of the creatures, eliciting a low mewling sound. Wil shudders. "This is going to be annoying."

From the staircase leading up to the common deck, Maxim says, "You know I'm not picking up poop, right?"

Wil looks up from halfway across the hold. "We can rock-paper-scissors-lizard-Spock for it."

"We will not. You cheat." The big Palorian turns and walks up the stairs ahead of Wil.

As Wil pushes the FTL throttle forward, he looks around.

"Who's feeding the Whatever They're Called, first?" As he asks, he taps a finger to his nose.

The other three crewmates follow suit as fast as possible; Cynthia is the slowest. She growls, looking at the two Palorians and human. "You all suck." Her gaze falls on Wil. "It's three days travel to the drop-off. The sofa in the lounge isn't very comfortable." When Wil opens his mouth, she adds, "It's also lonely being out there alone, you know. Just you...alone in bed. Just you."

Wil nods slowly, pressing a control to lock in the auto flight systems. "So, I'll go feed the Whatevers. One of you figure out dinner."

As the bridge hatch closes behind Wil, Maxim catches the two women sharing a look. "That's not right." He points at both of them. "You're not right." He gets up and heads for the bridge hatch as the two women laugh.

## CLEAN UP AISLE 42_

Three days later, in the now empty cargo hold, Zephyr looks at her hand. "In what galaxy did we sign up for cleaning?" She waves her hand toward the deck, trying to dislodge something purplish with hair in it. "Whatever the wurrin this is."

Maxim opens his mouth, but a sneeze from Cynthia kills whatever he is about to say. He looks at her. "What's wrong with you?"

She rubs her nose, small whiskers twitching. "I think I'm allergic to—" She looks around. "What were these again?"

Maxim leans against the bulkhead near the lowered cargo ramp. "Pallipsonnobs," he offers. He lifts his foot to examine the sole and grimaces. "Guess I can burn these."

Wil is standing halfway down the staircase connecting the common deck to the cargo hold. "This much shedding...Why do those hairy slugs have hair?" He continues down the steps, avoiding an especially hair glob of whatever it is the hair slugs excrete. "The client will be here in an hour." He points to something above Maxim's head. "Missed a spot." The big man makes a rude gesture. Wil turns to Cynthia. "You look like hell."

"I love you, too," she quips as she pushes a push broom toward a hairy purple glob. She sneezes and says, "Maybe we see about some type of liner for the hold or something." She waves to take in the entire hold. "Maybe something that can be washed."

"Or burned," Maxim offers.

Zephyr pushes her collection of hairy slime into the larger collection near the top of the cargo ramp. "Or we could just stop with the livestock jobs."

"Here." A loud, wet sounding sneeze. "Here," Cynthia adds.

Zephyr nods. "I'd be on board."

Maxim grunts. "Same. I hate these gigs."

Wil picks up a pry bar and uses it to scrape a hairy purple blob off the bulkhead near him. "We already talked about this. These gigs are easy money, and we're not overthrowing governments."

"Easy?" Cynthia said, her voice nasal and distorted.

Wil shrugs, grinning. "They can't all be save-the-GC-type jobs." He flings his pry bar toward the central slime collection, sending a glob sailing through the air. "Plus, those jobs always make my blood pressure go up. The auto-doc is surprisingly mean about health."

Maxim and Zephyr exchange a glance.

Cynthia walks over and rests a hand on Wil's not-entirely-flat stomach. When he looks down at her hand and back up, she says, "Just sayin'."

"Burn," Maxim says.

Wil scoops up a glob and throws it at the big Palorian. Before Maxim can retaliate, Wil dashes back up the stairs shouting and clapping his hands. "Good work, people! Keep it up!" His exit is punctuated by the sound of the hatch slamming closed above.

Zephyr turns to Cynthia, who is wiping her nose on her sleeve. The Palorian woman makes a face. Her Tygran friend says, "What? Allergies!" Zephyr points to the now closed hatch above. Cynthia looks up. "Oh, don't worry, he'll pay." She leans on her broom, shoving another several hairy purple globs into the main pile. "How are we going to get this big blob out of the hold?"

Zephyr smiles. "Oh, that's easy." She reaches for one of her pulse pistols, makes an adjustment, and takes aim. Her pistol makes a whining sound. Then she pulls the trigger. The energy bolt that leaps from the pistol is brighter and thicker than a normal pulse pistol blast. The purple hairy glob immediately ignites. As the blob sizzles, the loose hairs sticking out of it catch fire.

"Well, that's gross," Maxim observes.

The blob fizzles and spits as it burns. Zephyr steps back, holstering her pistol. "Okay, that's more gross than I expected it to be."

The blob pops loudly.

# CHAPTER 2_

# LONG DISTANCE CALL_

Wɪʟ ᴇɴᴛᴇʀs ᴛʜᴇ ʙʀɪᴅɢᴇ, still chuckling. He makes a stop at Cynthia's station, tapping a few controls. The primary display comes to life, showing a test pattern. Wil moves to his station and presses a control. The test pattern winks out, replaced by the face of an Asian woman in a military uniform. He smiles. "Hi. Wil Calder."

"Please hold." The screen changes to the logo of the Earth Government Alliance, a stylized globe with a triangle chevron behind it with smaller triangle swooshing around in front of the globe—like someone took the NASA and *Star Trek* logos and tossed them in a blender, then added Earth on top of it. Wil groans, looking at the image.

The logo vanishes, replaced with the smiling face of James Hawthorne. "Well, if it isn't the space pirate Roberts." He laughs. "Who'd have guessed an interstellar comm node is all it took to get calls from my dead friend?" James is in his office aboard the *Wil Calder*.

Wil returns the smile. "I mean, I'm also pulling the latest dump from my satellite, so figured I had some bandwidth to spare."

"Uh huh." The other man drawls, "What're you all up to?"

Wil waves a hand. "Oh, you know, saving the galaxy, stuff like that." He adjusts in his command chair, moving to lean back. "How are things there? How's the reconstruction?" He snaps his fingers. "How's the FTL trials?"

James whistles. "Things are better, more or less. The Alliance has ironed out a lot of the kinks overall. You heard they blamed the rampage on you, right? Or, rather, unspecified aliens." He uses air quotes for the last word.

Wil grunts. "Well, I suppose that makes sense." He frowns. "Heaven forbid they admit they kept an alien prisoner for a few years making him upgrade the U.S.'s infrastructure."

James nods. "Yeah, probably wouldn't go over well. Anyway, the reconstruction is going well. Lots of work to be done. Low unemployment is good for public opinion, you know." He looks off-camera, then turns back, beaming. "FTL trials are going well. We leave in a few days for a shakedown, out of the system."

"Dude, that's awesome!" Wil claps. "Congrats."

James inhales. "Yeah, the crew is pretty stoked. It'll be nice to be away from all the Earth First nonsense for a bit."

"Earth What, now?" Wil leans forward, his head tilting.

James looks around his office and leans closer to the camera. "Couple of months back, after the powers that be pinned the whole 'destroy America from orbit' thing on aliens, folks started rallying. At first it just seemed like a bunch of scared folks. I mean, suddenly there are aliens. Now it's a full-fledged movement. They believe humanity should stay on Earth, ban any alien contact, and eliminate any non-humans that set foot on the planet."

"Yikes."

"Yeah. They say it'll pass, but I'm not holding my breath." James grimaces.

Wil sighs. "Guess it's to be expected. First contact, such as it was, ended with a lot of death and destruction." The other man grunts his agreement. An indicator on Wil's console lights up. "Hey, man, I gotta bounce. Client is inbound."

"Your hauling livestock, huh?" James asks, then holds up a hand. "Maxim and I chat sometimes."

Wil groans. "Gotta pay them bills. Let me know how the FTL trial goes."

"Will do, my friend." The screen goes dark briefly, then resumes, showing a diagnostic or something. Wil has no idea. He brings up a keyboard on one of the displays in his console and taps a few commands into it. The diagnostic vanishes as a grid appears on screen. One by one, feeds from Earth-based news networks come to life, filling the screen, fed by Wil's satellite in orbit over his home world. At the bottom of the screen, the status of his download of media crawls from left to right.

He sighs as he expands one of the windows. A well-built, blonde-haired man in an extremely well-tailored suit speaks. "In other news, an Earth First rally in Toronto turned violent earlier today when counter protesters arrived. The Earth First crowd surged the police line, inciting a brawl that led to several arrests and a few hospitalizations."

Wil sighs as the video shrinks to fit back into the grid.

GETTING PAID_

When Wil comes down the stairs into the cargo hold, he whistles. "Well done, team."

"Stuff it," Maxim growls. He points out the large cargo doors. "Client inbound."

Wil walks through the massive cargo hatch and down the ramp. The Pallipsonnobs are in the temporary corral they had set up next to the ship. He steps off the ramp onto the dusty world they've been parked on for nearly six hours. In the distance, a heavy personnel transport is rumbling toward them on tank treads. The plume of dust it is kicking up rises dozens of meters in the air. "Showy," Wil murmurs as he turns to watch the hairy slugs in their pen, shuffling slowly this way and that. It looks like Max just fed them. The hairy nightmares were squishing around the pen after a dozen or so cantaloupe-like melons that their client had said they liked. Aboard the ship, they stuck with the kibbles the rancher gave them.

The transport rumbles to a stop a dozen meters from the *Ghost*, a door on the rear dropping to form a ramp. Three...well...cowboys descend. Hats, plaid shirts, and what look surprisingly like Levi's tucked into boots. The leader tips his hat. "You the Captain?" He is a muscular Trollack, tattoos covering his face. His pants have a cut out for his stubby fish tail.

Wil puts on his best smile. "Sure am. Wil Calder." He gestures to the *Ghost* and the crew leaning on the metal fence of the slug pen. "My crew. Well, some of them."

As the lead cowboy approaches Wil, the other two move off toward the slug pen. The leader looks at Wil, then the slugs. "Ugly, right?" He chuckles. He squints, his bulbous fishlike eyes wobbling a bit. "Don't I know you?"

Wil blushes. "Not that I know of." He turns to the pen, raising his arm, wristcomm display showing. "So, payment?"

The Trollack cowboy looks at his two companions. "They look all right?"

The taller of the two, a Malkorite, turns, his elephantine ears jingling as the various earrings sway. "Yeah, boss, they look fine. Looks like they all survived the trip." The third cowboy, another Malkorite, nods, causing his ears to set off a minor symphony.

The Trollack looks at Maxim and Zephyr, then back to Wil. "Hey." He takes a step back, his wobbly fishy eyes squinting. "Wait a microtock."

Wil puts one hand on the butt of his pistol, the other outstretched. "Payment, cowpoke?"

"Wait just a single...I know you guys!" He points a webbed finger at Wil. "Jowlow, Clembit! These are the folks who saved the Harrith system!" He looks up at the *Ghost*. "Holy wurrin, of course! That's the *Millennium Falcon*! You all helped the PKs blow up that monster spaceship, too!"

Wil glances at Zephyr, mouthing the word "*space*ship." She scowls.

One of the Malkorites—Wil has no idea if it's Jowlow or Clembit—says, "Well, I'll be. You all are famous."

Maxim groans. Cynthia sneezes. Zephyr clears her throat. "You know, we try to keep a low profile—"

The other Malkorite says, "What are you all doing hauling Pallip-sonnobs?" His friend bobs his head in agreement with the question.

This time Wil groans. "Like my first officer said, we like to keep a low profile." He wiggles his fingers, then holds his wristcomm clad forearm up, pointing at it. "Can we get to the money part?"

The Trollack blinks five or six times. Wil can't keep track. "Oh sure, sorry." He holds his own wristcomm up and taps a few things. Wil's unit beeps. "Think I could get an autograph?"

# HEY, OLD FRIEND(S)_

Cynthia blows her nose and says, "You're the one who's told me—us—more than once about the statues and childhood learning centers named after you." She reaches for another tissue. "Why are you peeved about that weird little man wanting an autograph?" They're sitting in their quarters after showering. The cowboys had asked for their help in getting the Pallipsonnobs aboard a ground transport that arrived after the cowboys paid the bill.

Wil ruffles his hair. "It's not the same. That stuff back home, it was all named after me because I was dead. I was famous, but dead famous." He makes a waving motion, taking in the *Ghost* and everything beyond. "We've saved the galaxy—"

"Just a part of it. The galaxy is big," Cynthia interrupts with a snort.

"Part of the galaxy—more than once. At best, we're a footnote. I dunno, feels shitty." He frowns. "Then he fucking tried to charge us for parking on his land."

Cynthia stands up. "You're weird. Get dressed and let's get off this rock." She presses the release on the hatch and exits into the corridor, closing the hatch behind her.

Wil is still in their quarters putting his boots on when the intercom chimes. "Hurry up, we've got a call." It's Cynthia.

"More slug transporting?" He stands and opens the hatch.

"More interesting—" a sneeze "—than those things."

THE BRIDGE HATCH OPENS AND WIL WALKS IN. THE MAIN display is on and he comes face to face with Barbara Mress, Chief Executive Officer of Tralgot Corporation, more recently the head of the GC task force in charge of dismantling Farsight Corporation's assets and unwinding the web of secrets and lies its former Chief Executive, Jark Asgar, wove.

"Oh. Uh...oh," Wil stammers.

"Eloquent," Mress quips, ears twitching. "Hello, Captain."

Wil looks at Cynthia sitting at her station. She shrugs. "We were catching up."

Wil walks to his command chair, putting his hand on the backrest. "Hi, Babs."

The Tygran woman smiles, her perfect teeth glinting. "It's been too long."

Wil drops into his seat. "So, what's up? How're things with Tralgot? It can't be summit time again. That was only a few months ago."

The older woman holds up a hand. "Tralgot is doing well, record profits this quarter. I'm still on Tarsis, actually, which is why I'm calling."

Wil leans forward. "Oh?" He glances to his right and sees Maxim and Zephyr also leaning a little closer to the large display at the front of the bridge.

"This isn't a popular idea, asking you for help," Mress starts.

"No offense taken," Wil deadpans.

Mress ignores him. "I can't give you many details over comms, but myself and several council members would appreciate your presence here. Your government needs you."

Wil doesn't blink. "Not my government."

# IT'S THE PRINCIPLE OF THE THING_

"Yes, well, whether or not you like it, the GC is *the* government, and they—we—I guess, could use your help," Mress presses.

Wil leans forward. "With?"

"With something I'm not at liberty to discuss over comms, as I said. Please, Captain, Wil, come to Tarsis. I'll explain everything. Your visit, of course, will be fully comped."

Out of the corner of his eye, Wil sees Zephyr frown and rub a hand down her face. He leans back in his seat. "Now you're speaking my language. It'll be a few days. We just finished a pretty important job in the Flintoh sector."

"Yes, hauling Pallipsonnobs. Cynthia told me." The older Tygran woman chuckles as Wil's face falls.

He looks over his shoulder mouthing, *traitor*. He turns back to the main display. "Anyhow, we're a few days out but are getting underway now."

Mress dips her head. "Very good. I look forward to seeing you all again." The screen goes black.

Wil turns to look at Cynthia, hitching a thumb toward the two laughing Palorians. "Them I expect to sell me out. You? Is nothing sacred?"

Cynthia bares her teeth. "Get us off this dren hole planet, please." She mimes blowing him a kiss.

Wil raises both middle fingers as he spins his chair in a full three-hundred-sixty-degree turn before settling in at his controls. He flips a few switches, causing a deep rumble to build. The sound builds and echoes through the ship as the reactor powers up. He looks up. "Hey... Damn. I keep forgetting Gabe and Bennie are on Arcadia."

Maxim grunts. "How can you forget that? The bridge doesn't smell like farts, and the sink is empty. A sure sign our little friend is off-ship."

"Truth," Zephyr agrees.

Wil makes some adjustments, then pushes the lever for the repulsor lifts forward, giving the engine nacelle-mounted devices power. The *Ghost* tilts a bit, then levels off as she rises off the prairie they had parked in to drop off the hairy slug creatures.

The *Ghost* lifts straight up until she is almost two hundred meters in the air. Wil checks the altimeter and says, "Hold on to your butts." He hears Zephyr sigh as he pushes another lever forward, this one controlling the atmospheric engines. The engines ignite with a deafening boom, and the small warship leaps forward on the ends of two fiery contrails.

Minutes later, the roar of the atmospheric engines dies out as the atmosphere thins. Wil pulls the throttle lever back towards him, cutting power to the engines. The *Ghost* keeps moving as he presses the sub-light engine ignition. Where the atmospheric engines roar, the sub-light engines thrum. There is a slight lurch, felt only in stomachs, as the sub-light drives kick in, taking over for the atmospheric engines.

"We'll be at FTL distance in a few," Wil announces as he spins his chair to face the back of the bridge. "Course is plotted. The auto flight system can handle it."

"You don't think Bennie will be mad we're not picking them up first?" Zephyr wonders as she puts her station into standby mode.

Wil shrugs. "I'm sure he'll be pissed, but it's not like Arcadia is on the way, and Babs made it sound like haste was important." He presses the control opening the hatch. "I could spar if anyone is game." Cynthia quirks an eyebrow and Wil smiles. "Someone said I needed to work out more."

Cynthia turns to Zephyr. "He's getting soft."

"Softer," Maxim quips.

"Squishy might be more accurate." Zephyr tries to keep a straight face.

Wil frowns. "You know, you all are mean. Very mean, mean girls and guy." He raises his middle finger and leaves the bridge.

Cynthia catches up to him halfway down the long corridor connecting the forward section of the *Ghost* with the larger main body. She drapes an arm around Wil's shoulders. "You know I love you, pudgy or not." When he growls, she laughs. "You're being a baby. You're not pudgy." She puts a hand on his stomach as they walk. "Or soft. Well, wholly soft." Before he answers, she adds, "Let's go spar, then get sweaty." She pats his butt as she opens the hatch to the common deck.

# CHAPTER 3_

# GETTING SWEATY_

"You're getting better," Cynthia says, stepping back from Wil. They're using padded bo staves. She twirls hers overhead and returns to a ready stance.

Wil is breathing much harder than her. "Thanks." He spins his own bo and sets his grip.

From the side of the training mat, Maxim leans over to Zephyr and whispers, "Who'd have guessed that the surly, borderline depressed human who sprung us would turn into," he points, "that guy?"

Zephyr nods, sitting up straight, inhaling her shoulders back. "He's come a long way, to be sure."

Maxim looks at her out of the corner of his eye. "Pride?"

"A little. I mean, he'd probably be dead if not for us. Either from the drinking or just pissing off the wrong person." She stands as Wil tumbles to the mat, his staff rolling to a stop in front of his first officer. She reaches down. "My turn?"

Wil looks up. "By all means." He stands and moves to leave the mat.

Cynthia smiles. "You did good, my love."

Wil smirks, looking at Zephyr. "Have fun." He drops onto the bench next to Maxim.

Zephyr kicks the bo staff into the air, catching it. Both women twirl their staves and square off.

Maxim nudges Wil. "I won't lie, it turns me on when they spar."

Wil looks at his big Palorian friend out of the corner of his eye. "A bit too much info, my friend." The big man shrugs without taking his eyes off the two women on the sparring mat.

Cynthia begins moving clockwise around the mat, her opponent doing the same. Without warning, she launches across the mat, bringing her staff up and around for a powerful overhead blow.

Zephyr moves just as fast, her bo staff blurring as it moves to intercept Cynthia's. The Palorian woman tilts, letting Cynthia's staff slide away. As part of the move, she spins, dropping her staff, letting it trail behind her. As she comes around, she whips her wrist, bringing the staff against her opponent's ankle just as she is trying to leap out of the way.

Maxim nudges Wil again. "That's my girl."

Wil leans away. "Okay, calm down, tiger."

Zephyr reaches down, offering her hand to Cynthia. They square off again.

Low enough so that their companions can't hear, Zephyr says, "Is it just me? Both of them are creeping me out, with the staring."

Cynthia circles. "Not just you." She turns to the men. "Cut it out, creeps." Both men lean back and find something on the ceiling of the cargo hold to focus their attention on.

Both women share a look, then focus on their sparring. This time it is Zephyr who takes the initiative, spinning her bo staff to lash out with a savage sideways attack. Cynthia brings her staff up and over her shoulder, turning to drop the staff down the length of her body, intercepting the blow.

The two women part. "I like that," Zephyr says.

Cynthia spins, letting her staff arc out and around in front of her.

Her tail swishes back and forth behind her as she moves. She grins. "It's important to get it right or your staff just slams into your ass."

# TRIP TO TARSIS_

"You ᴋɴᴏᴡ, I could get used to this," Maxim says. After sparring, the crew is grabbing a bite of dinner. The *Ghost* is scheduled to arrive at Tarsis in the morning. He takes a bite of his pizza.

"We really should have Bennie checked for worms or something," Zephyr says. "He's a fraction of our size and eats almost as much as Maxim." With Bennie and Gabe still on Arcadia, the rest of the crew has been making sure to eat the meals that Bennie usually ruins.

Wil wrinkles his nose. "And makes more gas." The other three laugh and enjoy the silence for a bit. Wil breaks the silence. "So, I got a new movie from my satellite over Earth, if you guys are game."

Maxim looks up from his slice. "You say that like it's something unusual." He grins. "Did you get new porn? Bennie will be mad if we watch it without him."

Wil blushes. "No. Well, maybe. That's not what I'm talking about, though." He shakes his head. "Wait, Bennie watches my porn?" He glances at Cynthia sitting next to him, staring expectantly at him. "That's...God, that's disturbing. Also, never have we and never will we watch porn as a group activity." He looks at his wrist-comm, shaking his head. "Anyway." He activates the entertainment display behind him on the bulkhead.

"What?" Maxim exclaims. "New *Black Panther?*" He grabs his plate, adding two more slices to it. He looks at the others. "Well? Come on." He turns and heads to the sofa.

Wil looks at the two women at the table with him. "Guess that's a yes." He stands.

Cynthia stands, adding a slice of pizza to her plate, as well. She leans over to Wil. "Feel free to queue up that new porn you mentioned for later." She slaps him on the rear end and goes to the large chair she usually shares with him.

Zephyr follows the group, watching people she would never have thought to call friend, let alone family.

"What about Tyr?" Wil asks. "We've never been. It's your home world and all." The two of them are lying in bed. They are en route to Tarsis, having finished dinner. It's four days to the capital of the Galactic Commonwealth, and there isn't much to do. Gabe stays on top of the maintenance checklist with a diligence Wil admires.

Cynthia props herself up on her elbow. "Uh, orphaned and put into a secret assassin training program. No, Tyr doesn't have a ton of good memories attached to it." She looks at the ceiling. "Plus, it's not very tropical or picturesque. It's just an industrialized world."

Wil puts his hands behind his head. "I mean, all planets have beaches, right? At least the ones with oceans."

"Does it have to be a beach?"

"Nope. Hell, I'd be happy for a few nights away from the peanut gallery, just us, on Fury," Wil says, then turns to his girlfriend. "But Fury is out. To be clear."

Cynthia tuts. "Yeah, we already spend too much time there, and now that we're putting down roots, yeah, Fury is out." She rests a hand on Wil's chest and says, "What about Earth? Your people know about non-humans now, even if they haven't seen many."

Wild shakes his head. "Yeah, no. For one thing, knowing about aliens and seeing a sexy cat-woman in a bikini on a lounge chair by the pool are two different things. For another, according to James, Earth is dealing with its usual closed-minded bigotry right now. Call themselves Earth First."

"That's a dumb name. First at what?" Cynthia asks, her feline nose twitching in what Wil knows is irritation.

"Who knows? Not space travel or extra solar colonization, that's for sure. I guess stupidity, maybe." He shrugs. "Earth is out."

Cynthia leans back, reaching for the small control panel next to the bed. She taps the control and lights go out. "Maybe Harrith? That resort was wonderful, at least what we got to see before...you know."

"An anti-us militia captured us and tried to kill us?" Wil adds.

She rolls over nearly on top of Wil. "Let's table this until tomorrow."

"Deal," Wil whispers.

## THIS PLACE NEEDS A BROTHEL_

"Gabe, you all need to make this place more exciting," Bennie says. He and Gabe are in the newly completed Arcology Two in the small studio Gabe is leasing. The city in a tower is nearly three kilometers tall, the uppermost floors lost in clouds. The droid nation has decided to leave as much of their world as untouched as possible, centering residential and commercial efforts into city sized towers. The two *Ghost* crew members have been on Arcadia for a week and half helping the provisional government get set up. After the vote in the GC Council, there was a bit of a mad scramble to secure the site for the first city, called, unimaginatively, in Bennie's opinion, First City. Bennie, having no interest in transporting livestock, volunteered to go with Gabe to Arcadia. He's been whining ever since. "I'm serious. This place is boring. You need a brothel or strip club, or something."

Gabe looks at his friend sitting on his impromptu bed in the corner of the sparse studio. Gabe, like every other citizen of Arcadia, has no need of a sleeping space, or a kitchen, or restroom, for that matter. Bennie has been vocal in his displeasure about these, in his words, "oversights."

"I fail to see what value such establishments would bring to Arcadia," Gabe replies from the floor-to-ceiling window he is standing next to. The window looks out on what will eventually be the government center and what will be called the Founders Park, a multi-acre green space dedicated to the early members of Gabe's movement.

Bennie joins his mechanical friend at the window. "I've been here a week and change. I can think of a few benefits." He looks from the view up to his friend. "I mean, this place is gonna welcome biologicals, right? We need things like toilets, beds, and most importantly, prostitutes."

"I do not believe sexual companions, particularly the for-hire variety, are in the pyramid of needs for biological entities," the droid retorts.

"You're not looking at the right pyramid," Bennie replies. Seeing that his argument is going nowhere, the Brailack hacker asks, "So, what's next on today's agenda?" They're at Gabe's place because it is one of the few places on Arcadia with a restroom right now, and after a hearty lunch courtesy of the recently installed food synthesizers, Bennie made his biological needs known to the work crew they were with. The sun is high in the sky, and while most citizens of Arcadia could work through the night, needing only a few tocks every few rotations to recharge, nearly all opted to keep a semi-diurnal cycle, for the benefit of biological visitors to the planet. Scant few there are, currently.

Gabe looks at his friend. "We are to join working group Omega Seven dash Fourteen. They are working on the network topography for this and the next two cities scheduled to go online."

Bennie lightly punches his friend in the thigh. "Let's get to it. I can't wait to dazzle..." He turns and looks at Gabe.

The droid makes a sigh-like sound and offers, "...working group Omega Seven dash Fourteen."

"Yeah, them," Bennie says, rubbing his hands together. "Network topography, exciting."

First City is only about thirty percent complete based on the initial, though ever-changing, plans that had been created and accepted by the provisional government. The interim governor, a squat power load lifter originally from Malkor, has seen fit to be very involved in the minutiae of civil design—to many of its provisional government members' chagrin, including Gabe's.

"GOOD MORNING. I'm Mon-El Furash, and I'm coming to you live from Arcadia." She smiles, her earrings jingling. "If that name isn't familiar to you, it will be. Arcadia is the new home world of the droid nation."

Behind her, a massive structure is being assembled. Mobile fabrication units are scaling the structure, printing sections as they climb. Droids of various shapes and sizes move about.

"Arcadia, until recently an unclaimed habitable colony world, will soon boast a population of thousands, possibly tens of thousands." She steps out of the way as a power load lifter stomps past.

"Excuse me," it rumbles.

Mon-El points, directing the camera pickup to a large cargo shuttle descending in the distance. "Emigration to Arcadia, for the time being, is under joint GC and droid nation control. Many systems have lodged complaints with the Galactic Commonwealth Governing Council over the expected mass shortage of labor."

She inclines her head. "The interim governing body of the droid nation has said that destabilizing GC members is not the intent of this fledgling new society and that they will work with the council and member systems to ensure as painless as possible a transition."

She grins. "I'm told the interim governor is also working on an official name for their society."

# CHAPTER 4_

## WELCOME (BACK) TO TARSIS_

"Peacekeeper corvette inbound," Zephyr announces. She looks up from her console at Wil sitting in his command and pilot's station.

"They're calling," Cynthia adds.

Wil points to the main display. A second later, the view of stars and the distant sun of the Tarsis star system is replaced by the stern countenance of a Peacekeeper commander. Her eyes narrow. "State your business."

Maxim chuckles quietly as Wil puts on a friendly face. "Hi! We're expected."

"By whom?"

"Uh, well, the Governing Council, I guess." Wil snaps his fingers, trying to recall a name. "Oh, Councilor Grythlorian maybe and Barbara Mress." He looks around the bridge. "I don't know if she has a title or something. Babs is definitely expecting us."

"Maintain your course," the commander growls before the screen turns to the logo of the Peacekeepers.

"She seems friendly," Wil quips as he turns to look at Cynthia. "Babs said she got us clearance, right?"

"They've really tightened security here," Maxim notes.

Cynthia looks from Maxim to Wil. "Yeah, her last message said she had cleared us for arrival." She glances at the chronometer set above the main display. "We're not early."

Before anyone can say anything else, the main display reverts to the Peacekeeper commander. "Light freighter *Ghost*, you're cleared through to Tarsis. Tarsis space control will guide you in." She doesn't wait for Wil to acknowledge, closing the channel.

On the main display, the Peacekeeper corvette veers off and resumes its patrol route. Wil looks over at his two Palorian friends. "I thought the Peacekeepers liked us now."

Maxim shrugs. "I'm sure after the Farsight thing, no one coming into Tarsis space is above suspicion."

Wil shrugs. "Yeah, I guess so." He pushes the sub-light throttle forward.

"Damn," Wil says as they arrive in orbit over Tarsis a few hours later. "Are there any Peacekeepers left in the rest of the GC?" On the main display, more ships than Wil can count are in various orbits around Tarsis: command carriers, corvettes and frigates, and everything in between. Wings of fighters weave between the warships and large freighters lumbering up and down the gravity well making their deliveries.

Zephyr looks up. "Yeah, that's a lot of firepower. I could understand that during the Farsight stuff, but that was over half a cycle ago." She looks at Maxim. "Shouldn't they be stood down by now?"

The Palorian man shrugs. "Obviously not." He consults his console. "And they're not shy about painting us, either."

Wil tunes them out as a screen on his console updates with their approved flight path. "Here we go," he says out loud to no one in particular. Ghostly green lines appear on the main display, showing their designated flight path.

Maxim watches the planet grow on the primary display. An older model heavy lift freighter slides past to disappear beyond the top of the screen. "Do we know what the plan is?"

Cynthia looks at the big man. "Are you tapped into the comms?" When he makes a face, she continues, watching Maxim out of the corner of her eye. "Just got a message from Ms. Mress. She's in meetings until tomorrow. We're to, and I quote, entertain ourselves without involving law enforcement." She laughs. "That was pretty fun, in hindsight. I was worried you idiots were gonna get sent to a penal colony. Anyway, docking clearances and the reservation for the hotel are included." She taps a few controls, and a window on the main display appears with the brochure image for the hotel where the Chief Executive of Tralgot has booked them rooms.

Wil whistles. "Okay, that's not bad."

The window closes as Cynthia says, "Looks like the course you're on is to their private spaceport."

On the main display, plasma streamers form and roll along the forward deflector shields. Between the clouds and super-heated air glowing against the shields, Wil can see the glow of the mega cities below.

# TEAM DINNER_

The *Ghost* sets down on her landing gear, hydraulics squeaking as her weight settles on the two articulated legs. Various vents near the gear expel gasses, the hull ticking and tinging as it cools. With a hiss, the cargo ramp lowers to the immaculate surface of the private spaceport.

"Damn, this is nice," Wil says as his feet hit the polished surface of the spaceport. He looks down. "Think they polish this daily?" He looks up, taking in the spaceport. The *Ghost* is only one of three ships parked in the spaceport, which could easily hold five more ships the size of the Ankarran Raptor.

Maxim and Zephyr join him, the big man adding his appraisal, "Wow."

Cynthia walks past them. "Come on, looky loos." She heads off toward an elaborate arched entry way.

Wil looks at the others and shrugs. "Onward." He heads off after the Tygran woman. He taps a few commands into his wristcomm, causing the *Ghost*'s cargo ramp to rise. Despite being on the most secure planet in the entire GC, he activates the security system.

THE RECEPTION AREA OF THE INTERPLANETARY IS NICER THAN any hotel lobby Wil has ever seen. "Damn," he whispers, suddenly self-conscious of how often he's been saying that. Cynthia is standing at a check-in desk talking to a Tarlack woman. She waves the others over.

"Hi," Wil says, reaching the counter. He puts a hand to his chest. "Wil Calder. I think you have rooms for us?"

The Tarlack woman looks at Cynthia, who clears her throat. "I, uh, already checked us in." She grins. "The reservation was in my name." Wil's cheeks redden. Cynthia puts a hand on his arm. "She likes me," she offers.

Wil frowns. "Whatever. Let's drop our gear and get dinner." He joins Maxim and Zephyr.

Cynthia looks at the Tarlack woman. "He's moody if he doesn't get fed regularly."

The other woman chuckles. "My partner can be like that, too. Enjoy your suite." As Cynthia turns, the woman adds, "Oh, if you need a recommendation for dinner, might I suggest the Slendo Flarn? It is highly rated, and only a short walk from here along sky path four." She points to an archway to the right of the check-in desk. Cynthia nods her thanks.

The suite turns out to be the penthouse. "Da—" Wil starts as he enters the central lounge. "— ng," he quickly finishes. Cynthia comes up behind him, followed by Maxim and Zephyr.

"This is nice," Maxim says, dropping his bag on the floor. He walks to the floor to ceiling window, putting his hand on the transparent material. Their rooms are several hundred meters up. He looks over his shoulder. "You said you had a reco for dinner?"

Cynthia nods. "Yeah, the woman at the check-in desk recommended someplace called the Slendo Flarn. I looked it up, looks good. Classy." She looks at Wil.

"What? I'm classy," Wil says, putting both hands on his chest. "I'm classy as fuck." He tosses his duffel on a sofa facing an entertainment screen. He looks at the others. "Hungry?"

Zephyr looks at her wristcomm. "Maybe a drink first?"

"Seconded," Maxim says, leaving the window. A gleaming shuttle passes by a few dozen meters beyond the window.

The sky path is bustling with Tarsi, Tarlack, and dozens of other species, most Wil recognizes by now, some he doesn't. A couple of what look like chihuahuas walking on vaguely human looking feet pass them by. Both are barefoot, yet otherwise dressed in smart-looking business attire. He watches them pass by, his mouth hanging open. One of the chihuahua people looks up. "Problem, baldy?"

Wil blinks. "Oh, uh." His hand moves to run through his hair. "What?"

Zephyr shoves him along. "Apologies." The male upright chihuahua glares but moves to catch up with its friends after making a rude gesture with equally human-like hands. Tiny human-like hands. She turns to Wil. "Tlebs tend to be short tempered."

"Heh, short," Wil says, looking over his shoulder at the group, now a hundred meters away. "I don't think I've ever seen a…" He looks at Zephyr.

"Tleb."

"A Tleb, before. Do they not get out much?" Wil continues.

Maxim says, "They don't like FTL travel." He shakes his head. "They hork." Wil grimaces.

Zephyr says, "I hear someone has released a medication to help them."

## TROUBLE FINDS US_

THE SLENDO FLARN is near the top of a towering commercial building. After some searching on the local network, Cynthia finds a few bars near the building. She picks one that sounds as un-seedy as possible, hoping to avoid any drama and law enforcement entanglements.

"Is this bar in a retirement community?" Wil asks, entering the space. The lighting is bright to the point of harshness. Tables and booths fill the space, there's no stage, and what sounds like Muzak filters in from ceiling-mounted speakers. He looks at Cynthia as she follows with Maxim and Zephyr. "You picked this place hoping we wouldn't get into trouble." It wasn't a question.

She grins and slides past Wil, heading for the bar. The bartender, a red-skinned four-armed man, smiles cordially. "Good evening," he booms. He looks past Cynthia to the rest of the crew. "Where you folks in from?" His lower pair of hands are absently wiping a mug with a frighteningly, to Wil, clean-looking cloth.

Cynthia grabs a stool and sits. "Four grum, please. We don't really have a home port; we go where work takes us." The rest of the group sits down, Wil to her right, Maxim and Zephyr to her left.

Wil adds, "But we did just buy our first place together. On Fury."

The bartender raises an eyebrow. "Wouldn't be my first choice, but congrats. Starting a family?"

Wil gestures to the two Palorians. "All four of us." When he sees the bartender's expression, he adds, "Oh, not a house, per se. A warehouse, for our business."

The bartender nods as he pulls four frosted mugs from a cooler under the bar. "I worked a long-haul freighter for a few years. Made me realize I like a planet under my feet. Visited Fury enough to know it wouldn't be Fury." He smiles, setting a frosty mug in front of each of them. His upper left hand salutes. "Enjoy." He doesn't wait for an answer, turning to offer a refill to an Ankarran woman a dozen stools away.

"Why is it so bright in here?" Zephyr wonders after taking a sip of her drink.

Cynthia gives her a feral grin. She points to a sign over the bar.

*Zero Tolerance.*
*No Warnings.*
*Behave, or Else!*

Maxim makes a noise, not a grunt, but similar. "There we go."

"Kinda boring," Wil says, then adds, "At least Bennie isn't here to complain."

Zephyr holds her mug up. "Cheers to that."

"Good afternoon. I'm Gulbar' Te."

"And I'm Belzar. Welcome to GNO News Time."

Gulbar' Te's long neck sways as he says, "Today we've got an update on the droid home world, Arcadia."

His co-host adds, "As well as an interesting and still unfolding story about mysterious ships being detected in a region known as the Void."

Gulbar' Te nods. "Very intriguing. First off, Arcadia. Interim Governor Mitch has released news that what we all have been calling the droid nation, have picked a name for themselves."

"How exciting," Belzar says.

The Burzzad newscaster bows his head. "Indeed. Citizens of the droid nation will now be known as Mechnoids."

"Bit of a tongues twister," Belzar quips.

"Indeed," Gulbar' Te agrees.

Belzar grins. "Well, congratulations to the Mechnoid people. Their contributions to the GC will be wonderful and numerous, I'm sure." He turns more serious. "Onto more ominous news. Several Peacekeeper ships have reported picking up mysterious vessels near the outskirts of GC space."

He turns to a different camera pickup. "The region known as the Void, which covers most of sector eighty-three by nine by twelve, is almost entirely devoid of planetary systems. Despite that, several ships are reporting seeing vessels on their long-range scanners."

"Is that so unusual?" Gulbar' Te asks.

Belzar shakes his head. "In and of itself, no, but the Void is not commonly traveled due to the risk of becoming stranded far from potential help. I'm told seeing the occasional ship isn't so rare, but seeing several is rare. The Peacekeepers are investigating."

"Good to know the Peacekeepers are on it," Gulbar' Te says.

"Agreed."

# CHAPTER 5_

# SO, THIS IS COMPLICATED..._

THE NEXT MORNING, an officious Tarlack man collects the crew of the *Ghost* at their hotel and escorts them to a glittering tower similar to the one where they'd met Councilor Grythlorian and her rude little henchman Blumtillithian. The shuttle they're riding in isn't quite as impressive as Tillith's.

Wil rubs his head and groans, "Space hangover." Zephyr sighs, rolling her eyes.

The shuttle sets down, and the side door slides open to reveal another four-legged being. This one, Wil now knows, is also Tarlack, like their escort. "Please follow me," the assistant to someone says and turns without waiting for them.

The waiting area is as luxurious as everything else Wil has seen on Tarsis. He turns to Zephyr. "Is there even a square kilometer of this planet that isn't swanky?"

She sits forward, the thumbs of her right hand tapping together as she thinks. "Well..." She turns to Maxim.

The big man huffs, "The underside. Pretty much dren all the way down, down there."

Zephyr nods. "True, I guess I don't count that part. Been tens of cycles since I've been down there."

"What's the underside? That sounds fun." Wil leans closer.

Cynthia chimes in, "It's not. It's the actual literal surface of the planet. What you probably think of as the ground is at least, what?" She looks at the others, doing math on her fingers. "A hundred meters above the actual surface."

Maxim nods. "Yeah, more or less that high."

Wil frowns. "What? Why?"

Before anyone can answer him, a door three meters tall swings inward on silent hinges. A Tarsi man in an immaculate suit appears. "This way, please." He steps aside, arm extended into the room he's welcoming them into.

Inside the meeting room is a conference table made of crystal, obsidian black crystal. At the head of the table sits Barbara Mress, head of Tralgot Corporation, and a Tarsi woman that Wil doesn't know. It's not Councilor Grythlorian. The two rise, and Mress comes around the table to welcome the crew of the *Ghost* warmly. She hugs Cynthia and grasps forearms with the two Palorians. Wil is set to mimic the gesture, the GC version of a handshake, when Barbara adjusts her grip to shake his hand. She smiles. "Captain Calder."

"Babs." He looks down at their clasped hands then up to her face, returning the smile.

As she turns to return to her seat, she says, "This is Councilor Selmak."

The Tarsi woman smiles, bowing her head. "Greetings, crew of the *Ghost*. It is an honor to meet you. Your exploits are quite well known, if not always appreciated by my colleagues."

Wil holds out a chair for Cynthia. "But appreciated by you?" Cynthia sits.

Selmak smiles again. "I take a more pragmatic view of the galaxy than my fellow Councilors." Maxim and Zephyr sit opposite Wil and Cynthia.

The room is dimly lit and windowless. Sconces three meters up the walls bathe the space in warm light.

The Tarsi woman nods to her Tygran companion. Mress clears

her throat. "We'd like to hire you. Someone has stolen data of a particularly sensitive nature."

Wil raises his hand. Selmak looks at him, eyebrow ridge arched. "Sounds internal. Why us? Why not PKs?"

Mress answers, "The data in question is Farsight data. In particular, research from one of the last stations to be discovered in our dismantling of Asgar's operations."

This time Maxim raises his hand. Selmak swats at the air, saying, "You need not raise your hands."

Maxim nods. "What kind of data? Who took it?"

Mress smiles, her sharp canine teeth showing. "I was getting to that. The data in question was contained on several portable data archives. It was more or less a complete backup of everything Farsight had learned about the Source creatures and their DNA." Wil guesses that's the official name for their friend The Source, and its monsters A through C. Mress continues, "The data, in the wrong hands, would allow someone to start Farsight's research anew, without the delay of starting from the beginning."

"So, they could make monsters," Cynthia says.

"Yes, though the creating of the hybrid creatures is not what concerns us," Selmak replies.

"Organic starship armor," Zephyr says.

The elder Tarsi woman dips her head. "The nature and process of building the armor Asgar covered his ships with is the thing we most fear right now. An armada of ships with biological armor plating would be a disaster."

## HAGGLE, HAGGLE_

WIL FROWNS. "Who stole these data arcs?"

Selmak gestures for Mress to continue. The Tygran woman inclines her head. "Have you heard of the Consortium?"

Maxim and Zephyr growl in unison. Wil looks across the table, then nods. "Yeah, we're familiar with them." Wil thinks back to Zarrix and the job where they broke into a secret deep space storage facility. At the time, they had no idea the Consortium controlled it or that, after they did the job, Zarrix would leak their identities to his pals in the Consortium upper echelon to ensure the blame didn't fall on him. They had worked their collective asses off for nearly a year to pay off the bounty the Consortium had put on their heads, since that was easier and safer than trying to set the record straight. Wil looks back across the table. "I'd forgotten all about them."

"We do less..." Zephyr looks at Mress and Selmak, "...legal adjacent work these days."

Wil leans back. "Yeah, those were fun days." Cynthia slaps a hand on his chest, almost knocking him backwards in his chair. "Oof." He sits up straight. "How'd they steal these arcs? Seems like something that important would be under guard."

"Or should have been destroyed immediately," Cynthia offers.

She wasn't part of the team when they'd stolen the crate that ended up containing a deactivated Gabe. She was working for Zarrix, though, and heard all about it from him, mostly via Lorath, his second in command.

Mress sighs. "They were on their way here to be locked in a vault. While the Council unanimously agreed to halt all Farsight research, they thought it best to keep the data locked away safely here on Tarsis, just in case. These arcs were a lucky find in that regard. Most of the Farsight facilities we found and raided during the early days of the dismantling were able to destroy their research before authorities arrived, in some cases setting it loose."

Wil shudders. "They let them loose?"

Mress nods. "Yes." She waves the thought of Farsight hybrid monsters running loose away. "The Consortium somehow found out and attacked the transport ship. We had hoped that an unmarked transport would attract less attention than a Peacekeeper convoy."

"You were wrong," Maxim surmises.

Mress and Selmak nod, the Tarsi woman saying, "We were. They raided the ship, killed everyone, and took the data arcs."

Cynthia leans forward. "This all sounds very..." she waves a hand vaguely around, "...special forces-y. We're not military." She nods to her Palorian friends. "Any more. Why us?"

"We're disposable," Zephyr says.

Selmak nods. "Yes, but that's not the principal reason."

"Not as reassuring as you may have thought," Wil says.

Selmak shrugs, continuing, "You're familiar with these Source creatures, for one thing. For another, you're not part of the GC government or military, which means the odds of this leaking to the news are slim." She looks at Maxim, then Zephyr. "And yes, you are disposable. If you fail, no one will know you're missing."

"Really not selling this," Wil says, adding, "We do have friends, you know." No one acknowledges him.

Mress adds, "Your team also has a knack for surviving unusual circumstances. That and your ties to the underworld should help you find the data arcs."

Selmak raises a hand to cut off the coming comments and questions. "Rest assured, you won't be doing this without support, matériel, and personnel."

"Okay, say we take this job. What's the pay?" Wil says. "We'll also have a shopping list, speaking of matériel support."

Mress smiles, nodding. "Of course. Additionally, we have certain assets at our disposal that may be of help, if you can figure out where the data arcs are being kept." She raises her arm, a delicate and expensive looking wristcomm on it. She taps the screen and swipes towards Wil. His own device beeps and he looks at the screen. He holds it up for Cynthia to see, then swipes to his Palorian crew across the table.

"We'll do it," Maxim says.

# THE ORIGINAL WAS BETTER_

THE CREW AGREES WITH MAXIM: the number on offer is enough to make the few worries they have not be that important. The upside of your client being the literal government of most of the known galaxy: deep pockets.

After a few hours going over details, where to meet resources and such, it turns out that the first person they have to meet up with is on Arcadia.

"At least we're not going out of our way," Wil says as the *Ghost* leaves the atmosphere of Tarsis two days later. The hold is full of equipment none of them are certain they'll need but will be useful later, for sure.

From her station, Cynthia adds, "We're cleared through to FTL distance."

Wil nods and looks at Maxim and Zephyr. "Did you two know the council had their own black ops teams?" He looks around. "Like, that's some seriously dark stuff."

Zephyr looks up. "News to me. I'd be willing to bet it'd be news to most Peacekeepers."

Maxim grunts. "Yeah, that definitely wasn't something that any

Peacekeeper I know was aware of. I'm sure the admiralty would have a..." He looks at Wil. "Bovine?"

"Cow, but yeah." He smiles. "I'd certainly hope so. I mean, damn, extra-military operatives?"

"That's one word for it," Zephyr mumbles, then adds, "By the way, the deposit cleared our holding account."

Wil beams. "Sweet. That'll help with the warehouse, for sure." He looks at his console. "Looks like twenty minutes to FTL." He turns to Cynthia. "Wanna let Bennie and Gabe know we're on our way?" She nods and turns to her console.

"You two settle on where you want to go on vacation?" Maxim asks as he settles onto the sofa next to Zephyr.

As she snuggles into her companion's side, the Palorian first officer adds, "I kinda like how roomy this sofa is without a certain Brailack taking up space."

Maxim grunts, "Right? How he takes up so much space despite being the smallest of us is beyond me."

Wil has Cynthia on his lap in the large overstuffed chair at a right angle to the sofa. He's got the control tablet for the entertainment screen in one hand and a bottle of grum in the other. Cynthia shifts to get comfortable and says, "Not yet. We've mostly narrowed it down by coming up with the places we do not want to vacation at."

"What about Ear—" Maxim starts.

Cynthia cuts him off. "Apparently having a bigotry problem at the moment."

Will groans, "Yeah, Earth is very much out. Though, if they get their shit together, there's a lot I want to show you." He looks up at Cynthia as she leans back against his shoulder, then to his two Palorian friends. "All of you."

Maxim nods. "I'm in no rush. No offense."

Wil laughs. "Yeah, none taken." He holds up the control tablet. "So, what's the verdict? New or old?"

"Old," Zephyr and Cynthia say, almost in unison. Maxim looks at them, then Wil. "I guess old."

Zephyr turns to look at him. "You like the new one? That male character, I just can't with him. They got the wrong...what's the term?"

"Actor," Wil volunteers.

"Actor for that role," she continues.

Wil nods. "Yeah, that was a mistake, for sure." He taps the tablet's screen and the movie starts. A few minutes in, LL Cool J is removing his face to reveal Drew Barrymore. The *Charlie's Angels* theme plays. Wil beams. "I do enjoy this version."

Maxim takes a sip of his grum. "So? Think Duch can help?"

Wil watches the movie a minute. "Hope so. He's never mentioned the Consortium, but neither did Zarrix."

Zephyr says, "He inherited Zarrix's empire. That must have included his connections to the Consortium."

Cynthia reaches over to tap the control tablet, pausing the movie. "It's kind of a rule of the Consortium: you don't talk about it."

"Like *Fight Club*," Wil says.

Cynthia ignores him. "Zarrix wasn't very high up in the organization. I can't see someone like Duch doing any better." She thinks. "But he definitely has contacts."

Zephyr takes a sip of her drink. "Worst case, he may be able to point us in the right direction. I can't imagine they're still using that station in the Barsoom sector."

Wil chuckles, remembering the heist. "Yeah, probably not. Would be bad for business." He resumes the movie. "Well, we'll hit Arcadia, then track down Duch and find out."

# CHECKING IN ON EARTH_

"Hey, loser." Wil smiles.

"It's Captain Loser, loser." James Hawthorne's face beams on the small comm unit display in Wil and Cynthia's quarters.

Wil bows his head. "My apologies, sir." Wil mock salutes.

"How're things in the dirty space underworld?" James is in his quarters aboard the *Wil Calder*.

"Oh, you know, grimy, space-y. How're things at home? That Earth First shit still going on?"

"Oh, yeah. They got a few of theirs elected to Congress," James says. "Several other member nations are dealing with them, too." He makes air quotes. "Make Earth Great Again..."

Wil groans. "Like a plague." James nods. "How're things aboard the...well, me?" He grins.

James returns the expression. "We're almost to Epsilon Eridani."

"What! Get out of town!" Wil slaps a hand on the small desk bolted to the bulkhead. "Congrats!"

James smiles, leaning back in his chair. "Thanks. So far, so good. They pushed up our launch a few weeks because of all the drama with those anti-alien morons." James moves to see past Wil into the room. "Where's Cynthia?"

"She's in the cargo hold. We're working on a mission. I needed a break."

"What kind of job? Saving the galaxy again?"

Wil laughs. "No. Something a little more pedestrian."

James grins. "Good, leave some of the fun galaxy saving stuff for the rest of us."

"Okay, Captain Kirk." Wil laughs.

James looks off camera, grimacing. "I gotta go, pal. Looks like someone in engineering hid their Earth First roots."

"You okay?"

"They subdued him." James leans forward. "Take care, don't get dead."

Wil nods. "Roger, roger." The screen goes dark.

# PART TWO

# CHAPTER 6_

# WELCOME TO ARCADIA_

THE SPACEPORT for First City is up there with some of the Tarsis spaceports on Wil's list of nicest places to land. Being barely a month old helps.

"Gabe says they'll meet us in the reception lobby," Cynthia says as the *Ghost* settles on its landing gear. She puts her station into standby mode and stands.

The others follow suit and head off of the bridge. As they walk down the corridor connecting the fore and aft section of the ship, Maxim runs a hand along the wall as they walk. "This place is pretty miraculous."

"The *Ghost*? It's taken you this long to recognize that?" Wil says through a smile.

The big Palorian shoves Wil lightly, still sending Wil colliding with the wall. "I mean Arcadia. A homeworld for droids. I'd have never thought I'd see something like this in my lifetime."

Zephyr pushes the control, opening the hatch into the common area. "Same. I'm glad it's happened but would not have given the idea good odds if you'd asked me ten cycles ago."

Wil smooths his t-shirt, tugging at make believe sleeves at his wrists. "Our boy is all growed up and a leader of men...well, sapient metal beings."

They make their way to the hatch leading to the stairwell that runs up and down the three decks of the Ankarran Raptor. Cynthia says, "I heard from a friend on Tyr that a lot of the droids there are applying to emigrate."

They descend the stairs into the cargo hold. "Yeah, GNO last night said droids from all over are applying. In record setting and distressing numbers," Zephyr says.

"Distressing?" Wil asks. The have spent the travel time organizing the cargo hold so that, despite their shopping trip on Tarsis, there is still room to move around. One corner has a crate Wil uses to store stuff from Earth in. The opposite corner, near the missile storage room, is packed with the newly acquired gear. He presses the controls on the small pedestal next to the large cargo doors. The doors grind as they slide apart, the cargo ramp lowering as they do.

"According to the news, several GC member systems are freaking out about the likely shortages in labor they'll experience if so many droids up and leave," Zephyr explains.

"Don't they have to agree to a work period to pay off their previous owner's investment in them?" Maxim asks.

"Yeah, but that appears to not be a big deterrent." Zephyr nods as they descend the cargo ramp. It's midday local time, and the *Ghost* is the only ship in the spaceport. "Gods, it's beautiful." She breathes. The spaceport hasn't collected the grime of centuries of engine exhaust and waste product being sloshed around. The duracrete still has a bit of a shine to it. Beyond the ring wall, two ovoid-shaped arcologies loom. A third, covered in scaffolding and massive cranes, is almost half completed.

"Think Gabe has a place in one of those?" Wil asks as the cargo ramp raises behind them, securing the *Ghost*. "What do droids need with apartments, anyway?" he wonders out loud.

"I asked Gabe that when he told us he was going to come to Arcadia to assist," Maxim offers. The pedestrian exit through ring wall is just ahead. "He said that the droids had decided to, in as many ways as possible, mimic other societies to make the rest of the GC feel more comfortable with them." He chuckles. "I don't think Bennie realized that while droids may choose to have an apartment for charging and such, they don't have a need for kitchens or restrooms."

"If he smells like a rotten onion, we're leaving him here," Wil says.

The tunnel through the spaceport wall ends a few meters in, exiting into a large reception area. On any other world, benches of waiting beings of all kinds would fill the space, waiting on friends and family arriving or saying goodbye to departures. Right now, it's empty save for a tall, shiny droid with a face still disturbingly similar to Maxim's and a Brailack that's moving from one foot to the other.

Gabe raises a hand, while Bennie rushes over to meet them. "Good to see you guys. I gotta get off this planet!" Bennie says excitedly. "These krebnacks are boring, and they don't have toilets!"

Maxim looks over to Wil. Both of them chuckle.

"Hello, my friends," Gabe says when they reach him. "It is good to see you all."

# GOVERNMENT WORK_

"So, then we had to debug the hydroponic control system in Arcology One, because even with thirteen landscaping droids on the team, none knew how to figure out the crop coefficient to avoid over-feeding." Bennie has been relating story after story of their two weeks on Arcadia ever since the *Ghost* landed. They're walking from the spaceport to the governmental building. "The worst part, it's so quiet here," he finishes, inhaling.

Gabe turns to his friends. "It has been anything but quiet since our arrival." Bennie sticks his tongue out, pulling one of his eyelids down.

The doors to the government building slide apart. Inside, the lobby looks a lot like the spaceport reception area. "We have focused on construction for the most part," Gabe offers. "Building interiors will be the last to be addressed. We do not anticipate many visitors in the near term."

"Makes sense," Maxim says, looking around the space. "Will be nice when it's done."

Gabe nods. "This way." He leads them into an amphitheater big enough for the *Ghost* to land in the bottom of. Gabe looks at his friends, noticing their awestruck faces. "While we work out the exact form of government that will represent us, for now all are welcome to be heard." He leads them along a spiraling ramp that cuts a path through the tiered levels naturally.

Wil notices that Gabe is pointing to what he thought was a powered down load lifter. It is a load lifter, but not powered down, just sitting motionless. It rumbles to life, shifting to turn its flat optical sensors toward Gabe and the others. "Hello, Gabe."

"Interim Governor Mitch," Gabe replies.

"Mitch?" Wil whispers to Cynthia, who elbows him in the ribs, then shrugs.

The load lifter droid rolls toward the group as they arrive at the bottom. "It is an honor to meet friends of Gabe the Liberator."

Gabe makes a choking sound. His friends all smile.

Zephyr inclines her head. "The honor is ours. You've accomplished so much in a short period."

"It helps that we do not sleep," Mitch replies. The load lifter is at least three meters tall and two wide. His scuffed and warn body is yellow with black stripes. "We expect to have phase one completed in forty or fifty rotations at the most." Wil whistles. Mitch continues, "We owe a great debt to Ben-Ari Vulvo. You might find this strange, but his technical skills rival that of many of our technical specialty citizens."

Bennie blushes a deeper green. He rocks on his heels. "My...uh... my pleasure."

Wil steps closer to the governor. "Listen, uh, Mitch, we actually have a favor to ask you."

Gabe tilts his head as he looks at Wil. Mitch can't nod, but answers, "If it is within our ability, the Mechnoid nation is at your service."

"We're looking for someone, one of your citizens. They would have emigrated here a month or so ago," Wil says. He adds, "They used to work for Farsight Corporation. Their designation was LK—"

Mitch raises a powerful forklift arm. "I know who you are speaking of. Their chosen name is Len. They have chosen to reside in

Arcology One, in the sublevel. They have chosen to forego the gender-based identifiers of our previous masters."

"The sublevel?" Gabe repeats, confused.

"I do not believe Len will choose to see you. When they arrived here, they made it clear they were seeking solitude. Not only from those who made them do unspeakable things—

biologicals—but from other mechanicals, as well. Hence the decision to establish their charging area in the sublevel." The interim governor adds, "I have not seen them since their arrival."

Cynthia nods. "All we can do is ask. The matter is of some importance." She turns to Gabe. "You mind being tour guide?"

Gabe looks from Mitch to Cynthia and back again before finally settling his optic sensors on the Tygran woman. "Of course. I am intrigued and wish to know more about our assignment." He turns to Mitch. "As always, Interim Governor, thank you for your time. I look forward to returning and seeing phase two well under way." He turns to the others. "Shall we?"

Wil waves to the interim governor. "Bye, Mitch. Nice to meet you." Under his breath he adds, "Mitch the load lifter. I feel like I'm in a children's show." Cynthia nudges him in the ribs again, eliciting a loud wheeze.

## THE GALAXY NEEDS YOUR HELP_

The sublevel of Arcology One is decidedly scarier than Wil expects. "Do you all shoot horror vids down here?" he asks as they leave the lift. It is nearly pitch black. He looks over his shoulder to where he thinks Gabe is and sees two yellow circles looking back at him.

"One moment," the droid says. The light panels come to life, bathing the entire sublevel in warm, natural light.

In a recharging alcove about as far from the lift as possible is a single droid. Matte gray, more or less humanoid shaped, similar to Gabe's original design, sans the second smaller set of arms. The head sports two oversized optical sensors, giving it a comical, shocked look. Wil is about to comment that the droid must be in standby mode when the optical sensors illuminate a brilliant blue. "Hello," they say.

The group approaches the droid. "Hi," Wil says, waving. "Are you Len?"

"Who else would they be?" Bennie asks. "You see other droids hiding in this basement?" Wil smacks him in the head.

The droid steps from their alcove. "I am. I was not expecting visitors today," they add. "Or ever," in a whisper.

Gabe steps forward. "Forgive our intrusion," he offers. "We have come to request your help." On the way over, Wil gave Gabe and Bennie the broad overview of the job.

"I have come to Arcadia for solitude and contemplation. I do not know what services I could offer you." They tilt their head, optical sensors spinning to focus on each of them in turn.

"It's about your former employer—" Cynthia starts but stops when Len raises both hands, palms out.

"I do not wish to relive my previous function. To that end, speaking of it is not something I will do."

Zephyr tries, "We understand—"

"You do not," Len interrupts.

"You worked for Farsight, we know," Wil presses. "We helped bring an end to what Asgar was doing."

Len's head tilts the opposite direction. "Then you have my thanks." They do not offer more.

Gabe says, "Perhaps if I try." He says nothing else, standing perfectly still, looking right at Len.

Wil opens his mouth but stops when Bennie rests a hand on his arm. "This is what they do. Communicate wirelessly. Way faster than vocalizing and they know it drives us nuts." Wil looks down at his friend and smiles knowing how much Bennie hates to be excluded from things.

Gabe stirs a moment later. "Len will accompany us."

"They will?" Maxim asks.

"I will," Len affirms.

As they walk up the cargo ramp, Wil looks over at Len. "Uh, would you like to set up in one of the guest berths, or...?"

The droid turns their head to Wil, then to Gabe. Gabe says, "You may utilize engineering if you like." Len nods.

Wil slows down as the matte gray droid heads into the cargo hold. He looks up at Gabe, a question on his face.

"Len is not comfortable with biologicals."

Wil turns to watch the enigmatic droid move further into the cargo hold. He looks back at Gabe. "Why? I mean, Mress told us he worked for Farsight, at the last research facility to be shut down. Was he abused?" His face darkens at the thought.

Gabe stops, forcing Wil to do the same. "No, Captain. From what Len told me, they feel deep remorse for their part in the experiments conducted at the research facility. They sacrificed hundreds of beings to the hybridization project." Gabe resumes his pace up the cargo ramp. The others are moving up the stairwell to the common deck, Len with them. Gabe continues, "It was their hope to find solitude on Arcadia and never have to be near those they caused so much harm to."

Wil nods slowly. "I'll let the others know. We'll give Len the space they need, when and where we can. I don't want this trip to be too painful for them."

"Your concern is appreciated. I will let them know."

A few minutes later, as Arcadia falls away from the *Ghost* on the small, rear facing camera window set on the primary display, Cynthia says, "I've got Duch."

Wil takes a deep breath, letting it out slowly. He nods and the screen changes to a view of a blonde-haired surfer bum whose grin reaches ear to ear. "Hi, guys!" The outwardly happy-go-lucky crime boss waves. "What's up?" In the background, Grell and Zash are arguing about something. The short, purple, ape-like being is flailing excitedly.

Wil puts a fake smile on. "Hey, buddy! We were wondering if you were too busy for guests? We've got something we wanted to pick your brain on." When he notices the other man's smile falter, he adds, "And it's been way too long since we've seen you. Zephyr misses ya." Out of the corner of his eye, he sees his first officer slump in her chair, grimacing.

Rhys Duch, one-time nobody in Xarrix's criminal empire, now the head of said empire, beams. "Of course! Always time for my friends. I'll have Grell send the coordinates! We're not on Crildon Three."

# NEWSCAST_

"Hello, I'm Xyrzix, and this is GNO News Break. Good evening." The blue-skinned newscaster smiles. "Today we're covering the launch of the *Galactic Empress*, the newest cruise ship from Red Nova Cruise Lines."

An image appears of a massive starship nearly as big as a Peacekeeper Command Carrier.

"The *Galactic Empress* is fifteen percent larger than her sister ships in the Red Nova fleet. I'm told she'll be leaving dry dock in another half cycle, able to carry five thousand passengers."

An image of a grand atrium appears. "According to the Red Nova spokesperson, the *Empress* will be like nothing else in the GC. Her initial route will be a tour of the some of the wonders of the GC, culminating in the Moklan private pleasure station, owned in part by Red Nova."

The images vanish. "Join us tomorrow. My colleague Klor'Tillen will broadcast live from the Red Nova dry dock for a tour of the shipworks."

# CHAPTER 7_

## SHADY FRIENDS_

When Rhys Duch isn't running his criminal empire from Crildon Three, he runs it from a personal yacht that has every jaw on the bridge of the *Ghost* hanging open.

Wil looks over his shoulder. "I never saw Zarrix use that."

"Zarrix didn't own that. That's a new addition to the fleet," Cynthia replies. She is staring past Wil to the majestic vessel directly ahead of them. If someone were to take a great white shark and cover it in hull plating, adding engine nacelles to its tail, that would come close to Duch's yacht. There isn't a right angle to be seen on the massive vessel. While Wil is certain the ship isn't designed for the water, he is equally certain it would do well in it. Twin nacelles are mounted at the ends of the large tail fin, equidistant from the ship's centerline. The shark analogy falls down where fins are concerned; Duch's ship has them, more of them than a shark. They seem to house maneuvering thrusters and sensors. The dorsal fin has a wrap-around window about halfway up its height.

Where gills might be on a shark, a large open hangar passes through the ship, static atmosphere barriers glittering as they keep the atmosphere in.

Cynthia looks down at her console as she puts a hand to her ear. "We're cleared to land."

Wil nods, making course corrections. "You know, he's starting to really make me rethink some of our career choices." The large vessel looms larger and larger, the hangar now taking up almost the entire primary display.

From his station, Bennie says, "Makes me think Duch is making up for something."

Maxim stifles a laugh. Wil grins. On the display, the static atmosphere barrier twinkles.

The hangar is empty except for the *Ghost*. While the port and starboard portals are big, the actual hangar stretches aft another hundred meters of the overall roughly five-hundred-meter-long, shark-shaped vessel.

The *Ghost*'s cargo ramp makes a metallic clang as it strikes the deck of the spacious hangar.

Grell is standing a dozen meters away. "Hi, gahs!" the purple being drawls as he trots toward them. "So glahd to see you. Bahss is waiting in his office."

Wil turns to the others, smiling. Grell hasn't changed. "Lead the way, grape ape." The short purple being rubs his chin, then shrugs and heads toward a hatch in the wall.

They fall in behind the excited, long-armed, purple being. Wil looks over his shoulder as the cargo ramp rises to seal the *Ghost* back up. Len is still aboard, but Wil has no idea if the bot would defend the ship or if they even have the ability.

"So, Grell," Cynthia says, "what's the deal with this thing?" She waves both arms to encompass the hangar. "This must be new. Zarrix didn't have anything like this, that I recall."

Grell pushes a button to summon a lift and looks up at Cynthia. "Duch got this, oh..." He taps a meaty finger against his temple. "...

About a cycle ahgo, I guess. One of thah ladies in charge of the Skai Lora sector protection racket cahme across it. Duch liked it, so..." He trails off. The lift doors open and everyone files in.

When the doors part, they reveal an impressive reception area covered in thick carpet and dark woods. Wil whistles. Grell looks up, grinning. "Raght?" The purple man points towards a door in the forward bulkhead. "Through thahr."

THE WRAPAROUND WINDOWS THEY SAW ON THE DORSAL FIN OF the shark ship is Duch's private office. The view behind him is the expanse of space ahead of the ship, below the graceful white lines of the vessel.

The gangster rises. "What do you think?" He makes a slow turn as he comes around his desk.

Maxim takes Duch's offered arm. "You have a beautiful ship, Duch."

Bennie nods, stepping up to exchange greetings. "Yeah, this thing is really impressive." The Multonae man looks like he might explode from an overabundance of pride.

Wil smiles. "Bet this intimidates the subordinates." He grasps Duch's forearm.

Duch bobs his head. "It really does. I drop out of FTL and folks start calling in their apologies for missing a payment." He motions to the array of sofas and chairs set near the starboard side of the office in a conversation space. "So, you wanted to talk to me about something?"

## BAD HOMBRES_

"The Consortium? Oh, wow. They're terrible folks." Rhys Duch sits forward in his chair. "I try not to get involved with them. When I took over Zarrix's operation, I stopped paying dues." He looks around the gathered crew of the *Ghost*. "Didn't you all have a run in with them? I remember the bounty bulletins."

Wil frowns. "That was a misunderstanding."

"You didn't rob them?"

Zephyr makes a noise. Wil glares at her. "Well, we did, but Zarrix paid us to do it."

"Not fully," Bennie grumbles. Wil nods.

Cynthia jumps in, "Anyway. We need to know everything we can about them, particularly where they may keep things they...you know."

"Steal?" Duch offers. Cynthia nods. He sighs. "Okay, I'll tell you all what I know, for..." He looks at the ceiling, "...two percent of whatever you're being paid."

"You son of a—" Bennie starts.

Wil holds up a hand. "Deal." He glares at Bennie.

Duch presses a control set in the arm of his chair. "Hey, Grell? We're gonna need snacks."

"And drinks," Wil says loud enough for the purple man to hear over the comms.

"And drinks," Duch adds. He turns back to his guests. "I guess you should start with what you're looking for."

Wil clears his throat. "We don't yet have all the details, but here's what we know."

"SOUNDS LIKE THE CONSORTIUM, ALL RIGHT," DUCH SAYS after Wil finishes. Grell has dropped off the snacks and drinks. Duch sips his drink. It's pink. "I know they decommissioned the station you robbed. It's been a few cycles now since I stopped paying, so they may have moved or decommissioned others, but if I had to bet, I'd say the station with your data arcs is likely the one they call Naetu."

"Oh, that's not disconcerting at all," Maxim quips. Wil looks at him, a question on the tip of his tongue. Maxim says, "Hell or the underworld."

Duch looks at Maxim and continues, "Yeah, it's aptly named. It's a space station, I think about twice or more the size of the one you robbed. It's deep down well of a system with a blue star. The radiation and heat are such that specially designed shield ships have to escort smaller vessels in. The station has a massive...I guess you'd call it an umbrella, where ships park, protected from the star's heat and radiation."

"Sounds tricky," Zephyr says.

Duch nods. "Yeah, and I don't think the trick you used to get into the Barsoom station will work. Zarrix may have played you, but the Consortium never quite trusted him after that break in. They changed everything about their security procedures."

"You have the procedures?" Wil asks.

Duch thinks a few seconds. "Yeah, probably. Maybe?" He stands and goes behind his desk. A terminal screen rises from the surface.

He taps a keyboard. "Here we go." He presses a button, and Wil's wristcomm chimes.

Duch returns to the chair. "I gotta say, guys, I don't like your odds."

"Thanks," Wil deadpans.

Duch shakes his head. "I'm serious. I like you guys, and let's be honest, you got lucky last time."

"Insulting," Maxim grumbles.

Duch presses on. "You had insider knowledge courtesy of Zarrix. You knew where to go and had the means of finding what you were looking for." As the crew of the *Ghost* nods along, he adds, "Do you have any of that here?" Wil and the team exchange awkward looks. "Exactly," Duch concludes.

Maxim stands. "This is reassuring." He walks to the nearest transparent section of the hull, looking out.

Wil watches his friend, then turns to Duch. "Any reason to think you could get back into the Consortium? Set up an account or whatever? Rent a storage unit?"

The Multonae man barks a laugh. "I like you, but not that much." He shakes his head. "Those guys terrify me."

Bennie tilts his head. "Aren't you, like, as powerful as Zarrix was?"

"More. I've expanded operations nearly thirty percent."

"And you're afraid of the Consortium?"

"Tells you something, huh?" Duch replies.

# GETTING SETTLED_

Rhys Duch treats the crew to a meal before sending them on their way. He has business to "deal with elsewhere." Wil chooses not to ask for details. The *Ghost* slides out of the static atmosphere barrier and powers up her sub-light engines. The distance between the two ships grows until the massive shark vessel turns and jumps to FTL.

"So, what now?" Maxim asks, looking up from his station.

Gabe, standing next to the bridge hatch, says, "I will speak with Len." He turns and leaves.

Wil watches the hatch slide closed, then says, "I guess we wait." He turns back to his console. They're in deep space, light years from any system or station. "This is as good a place as any to sit." He looks around. "Combat Sim?"

"Haven't done that in a while," Zephyr says. She's smiling.

Maxim cracks his knuckles. "I'm game."

Bennie turns. "How about the one with the *Star Wars* ships?"

Wil laughs. "Sure."

"Greetings, Len," Gabe says as he enters engineering. The matte gray droid is standing near the main control console watching a diagnostic run.

They turn. "Hello, Gabe. Was your visit with the criminals fruitful?"

Gabe inclines his head. "To a degree. We believe we know the likely location of the data archives."

"That is good. You will return to Arcadia to drop me off?" The bright optical sensors spin as they focus, whirring slightly.

"I am afraid not. Not yet, at least. We must figure out a means by which to gain access to the stronghold where the archives are being kept."

"I fail to see..." Len tilts their head as if they're listening to something, then turns to the main console. "Can I access the internex from this terminal?"

"Yes."

Gabe watches the research droid work the controls of the master engineering console. As a precaution, he has not given Len shipboard wireless network access.

Several minutes later, the other droid turns. "I believe I may have information that will be of use." He strides towards Gabe. "I should address your crew."

"Are you certain you are comfortable with that?"

"Not even a little."

"Three inbound, starboard low!" Zephyr is shouting as the bridge hatch opens to admit Gabe and Len. On the main display, three TIE Interceptors from *Star Wars* zip past.

Wil leans into the flight controls as Maxim shouts, "I need a better angle."

"On it!" Wil says. He pushes against the controls. On the

primary display, the stars are spinning wildly as energy weapons' fire flashes.

"I do not understand," Len says in a low tone.

"Combat simulation," Gabe offers.

Cynthia looks up. "Oh, hey!" She presses a glowing red button on her console. The bridge lights return to normal in a blink as the enemy vessels on primary display freeze in place.

Wil turns. "What's up?"

Gabe inclines his head towards Len. "Len believes they may be able to shed some light on our current predicament."

Wil stands. "This sounds like a conversation for more comfortable seats." He extends an arm toward the hatch behind the two droids.

Once bottles of grum are in hand, Wil looks at the two droids standing near the main entertainment display. He drops onto the arm of the large chair where Cynthia is sitting. "Lay it on us."

Len looks at Gabe, who nods. The dull gray droid turns to face the crew. "Gabe informed me of your current predicament. I believe I may have information that could ultimately help."

Maxim leans forward. "What ya got?"

"During my time with Farsight, I was assigned to several research stations. The GC team in charge of dismantling Farsight found me and my team on Station Forty-Two. However, research station Meltrom was perhaps the most important of my assignments. It was certainly the most secretive. I confirmed with public records that it is listed as destroyed."

"Destroyed is good?" Wil asks.

"Destroyed would be good, yes. However, I was on that station in the last cycle, and it was very much not destroyed," Len replies. "I believe Farsight, in their final moments, marked the station destroyed in order to keep Galactic Commonwealth officials from discovering it."

Bennie taps a PADD he has with him; the main entertainment

display comes to life. On it is a split screen view of public records and data Mress gave them from the Farsight Commission. Both sets of data claim that the station was destroyed nearly four cycles ago, never taking part in Farsight's hybrid Source monster project. "Huh," he says.

Maxim looks at his small friend. "Good huh, or bad huh?"

Bennie looks up. He's grinning. "Clever huh."

# BAD RECORD KEEPING_

Len continues, "Not only is the station still there, it was home to several..." If it is possible for a droid to convey being uncomfortable, Len is doing it. "...Experiments. The station was a clearing house for the more successful experiments. I cannot be certain, but one such experiment may be valuable to your mission."

Wil opens his mouth, turning to Bennie, who says, "Course is already on your console on the bridge."

Wil closes his mouth then stands up. "Be right back."

Cynthia looks at Len. "Thank you for sharing this with us." Len makes a noise but says nothing. Cynthia adds, "You are not responsible for this. Especially for things that happened before you could make your own decisions."

Bennie chimes in, "She's right. If I'm not mistaken—and come on, when am I ever? —

research droids aren't loaded with an excess of empathy or other emotional constraints that might hamper your objectivity in research."

Len says nothing, then finally, "I appreciate your words. While you are technically correct, it does not alter my perception." They turn and head for the short corridor leading to engineering.

Wil returns. "We're on our way, looks like three days." He looks around. "What happened to Len?" Gabe points down the corridor.

MAXIM IS PANTING. "YOU'RE GETTING GOOD." HE TAKES A FEW steps back, kicking his bokken up to catch it. He twirls the wooden practice sword as he turns to face his opponent.

"Thanks. The training materials C7K2 sent have been tremendously helpful," Bennie says. He and Maxim have been sparring several times a week since returning from Nexum. Bennie twirls his bokken. "Another round?" He assumes a ready stance, wooden blade held backwards in his right hand behind him, his left angled out in front of him.

Maxim smiles. "One more." He lunges in, swiping sideways with his bokken. Bennie takes a step back, bringing his weapon up in an arc to deflect Maxim's much more powerful blow, deflecting the energy away from the much smaller Brailack. The bigger man smiles as he steps to the side just in time to parry his opponent's downward slash.

Bennie leaps backward, bringing his bokken up into a guard position as Maxim makes a backward slash, hoping to catch his nimble opponent by surprise. "Almost!" the Brailack huffs.

The two square off again. This time Bennie launches the first attack, moving quickly, hunched forward, his wooden blade held low. He slashes upward, trying to get in under Maxim's defense, but is brought up short by a thick blue hand pressing against his chest, shoving him away.

Bennie lands and looks up as a bokken levels at his face. He bats the wooden sword away. "Sneaky." He holds out his hand. Maxim helps him up.

"All's fair," the big Palorian says as he hauls Bennie up to his feet. "Sir Jarek Ruus would be proud."

Bennie beams. "That means a lot, thanks." He walks to the edge of the mat and picks up a pair of towels, tossing one to Maxim.

From the overhead speaker, Wil announces, "Dinner, assholes." Maxim looks at Bennie and grins. They stow their training weapons and head for the staircase.

When they arrive on the common deck, Wil is setting the table, while Zephyr is working at the cooktop. Cynthia is already at the table watching Wil work. She turns to Maxim and Bennie. "Yeah, showers, please."

"It can't be that bad," Bennie starts to protest but is cut off by Cynthia's expression.

She points to her nose. "Way more sensitive." Maxim puts a hand on his small friend's head and turns him towards the berths.

Wil drops into the seat next to Cynthia. "Good call. Ripe Brailack is truly horrible." She nods her agreement.

# THESE ARE THE VOYAGES_

"How's the weather?" Wil asks. He's lounging on the common deck with Cynthia while everyone else busies themselves elsewhere. They're sitting on the sofa looking at the larger-than-life face of James Hawthorne on the wall-mounted entertainment screen.

"Dusty." He grins. "The debris rings are incredible. Like nothing in our system. You can literally see the belt with the naked eye." He's leaning forward in his seat, his eyes bright. "We're only gonna be here a few days, sadly."

"Now who's Captain Kirking?"

"Kirk-ing?" Cynthia repeats, emphasizing the wrong part of the word.

James laughs. "Don't let her get away."

Cynthia smirks. "As if he could. It's good to see you, by the way."

"You, too," the dark-skinned man replies. His eyes shift slightly, looking at Wil. "We found quite a few things that need a little fine tuning."

"Anything serious?" Wil shifts slightly, getting more comfortable as Cynthia leans into him.

James shakes his head. "Nah, mostly just things that wiggled loose here and there. Our little Earth Firster ensign didn't get a chance to cause much damage." He sighs. "Taking the win where I can."

"Find any others?" Cynthia asks. When James raises an eyebrow, "Wil told me about your bigot problem."

James mulls over the phrase. "Bigot problem, I like it. Yeah, no other Earth Firsters have been found among the crew. I heard from Command that they're causing all sorts of trouble back home. India, China, the Europeans, all having issues."

"Great googa mooga," Wil murmurs.

"Yeah." James looks off camera, then turns back. "Gotta go. We just confirmed that the second planet is here, and get this. In the Goldilocks zone."

"What?" Wil leans forward, nearly shoving Cynthia aside.

His longtime friend beams. "Right?" He winks and the wall display goes black.

Cynthia turns to Wil. "Goldilocks?"

Wil laughs, pulling her close. "The habitable zone."

"Ah."

# CHAPTER 8_

## ONLY THE NICEST PLACES_

"Well, this seems welcoming," Bennie says as they approach Farsight Corporation Research Station Meltrom. The station is sitting at a Lagrange point between a rocky atmosphere-less planet and the system's star, a red dwarf.

Wil watches the station grow. "That's a piece of shit."

Len, standing next to Gabe at the bridge hatch, leans over. "He has a colorful vocabulary."

"You have no idea."

The station is nearly a kilometer long, tapered at one end. The wider end has a rectangular opening leading to a hangar bay. Several spines radiate out from the cylindrical station.

Zephyr is leaning over a screen on her console. She looks up and back to the two droids. "I'm not picking up life signs."

"You would not. He is there."

Wil makes adjustments to their course. "Any signs that anyone has been here recently?"

Zephyr shakes her head. "Not that I can see."

"No sign of weapons, targeting sensors—well, sensors of any kind," Maxim reports.

"I am seeing power, though," Zephyr adds.

On the large display at the front of the bridge, the dilapidated station keeps growing. At this distance they can see that several hull panels are missing, antenna masts are bent, what looks like a docking tube is raggedly drifting, still attached to an airlock midway along the port side of the station.

Wil points to it. "Someone was here."

"Not recently, by the look of it," Bennie says.

The station takes up most of the primary display. Wil guides the *Ghost* around the station in a lazy circle several hundred meters out. The forward flood lights blaze, illuminating the darkened side of the station.

Wil looks over his shoulder. "You said you were stationed here a year ago?"

"One point one two cycles ago," Len answers.

"Shit's gone downhill fast," Wil says.

"Captain, I believe some of this damage may be intentional," Gabe says. Wirelessly, he instructs the camera to pan towards a section of damage, a missing hull panel. The hole looks ragged, but the equipment underneath is carefully adjusted to remain undamaged.

"Len's boogeyman wants people to think this is space junk," Maxim says.

"He did a good job," Cynthia offers. "I've been hailing the station. Nothing."

Wil brings the ship board toward the front of the station and gaping hangar bay. "Any reason we shouldn't use the front door?"

"None that I can think of," Len offers.

The *Ghost* slides inside the darkened bay. With little to no power, there is not a static atmosphere barrier, lights, or gravity. The *Ghost*'s flood lights do a reasonable job illuminating the space.

"Cozy," Cynthia says, watching the far wall of the bay grow closer. The bay is empty aside for a few scattered and open cargo crates. No ships or shuttles are present.

The *Ghost* settles to the deck, her landing gear magnetizing to keep the ship to the deck.

"Guess Len's friend doesn't need gravity," Zephyr says, putting her station into standby mode. Everyone follows suit.

Wil says, "All right, Len and Gabe, why don't you meet us in the cargo bay? We've got to get dressed." The two droids nod.

With all five biological members of the crew in the armory at the same time, it is cramped. "Get your ass out of my face!" Bennie pushes Wil away from him. Wil almost falls over.

"Stop being ass height, then!" Wil growls.

Cynthia laughs as she watches Wil pitch forward trying to right himself, one leg trapped halfway into his insulating undergarment.

Maxim has dragged most of his gear into the area just outside the armory. "Thinking next time someone is willing to foot the bill on modifications, we expand the armory."

Wil straightens, slipping his arms into the close-fitting garment. "Agreed." He turns to glare at Bennie. "Maybe our green asshole gets dressed in an airlock."

"Try it, pinky," Bennie growls, his hand resting on his beam saber.

Zephyr looks at the two them. "Can you two relax? This would be easier if there were less pushing and shoving."

"He started—" Bennie says.

"I will shoot you, right here on the spot," Zephyr interrupts, hand on the butt of one of her pulse pistols. She's more than half into her armor.

# DO WE DO RERUNS?_

THE CARGO RAMP DROPS, soundlessly hitting the deck of the dark landing bay. Gabe and Maxim lead the way, the former in his combat mode. Len and the rest of the crew follow, Zephyr and Wil bringing up the rear, their rifles held at the ready.

"Jarvis, deploy the ducks," Wil says as he steps off the ramp, his armored boots securing themselves to the deck.

"Of course, sir," the chipper, vaguely British-sounding AI replies. From the backpack built into Wil's armor, four small spheres each about the size of a softball pop out. Each is painted a different color, much of the paint scuffed. The spheres drift for a few seconds, then orient themselves and shoot off toward the half open hatch at the far end of the bay. "I'll monitor the ducklings and Launchpad and let you know if they find anything," Jarvis offers. "However, right now, they are stuck. The inner doors of the airlock are understandably sealed."

Wil nods to himself. "First order of business: let's get the airlock working."

Gabe shifts out of his combat mode, his forearms shifting and changing, blasters moving back into his arms as his hands take form. He moves ahead of them toward the airlock doors. Over the comms, he says, "Someone has tampered with the outer doors. The damage is repairable."

Bennie edges around his mechanical friend, then gestures to the bay and the station beyond. "Lotta work went into making this place look broke down and uninviting." Nods all around acknowledge the observation.

The airlock doors shift, their clunking motion traveling through the deck to everyone's boots. Gabe looks up. "I was wrong. I cannot fix this."

"Oh well, we tried," Bennie says, turning to head back to the *Ghost*.

Maxim reaches out and grasps the helmeted head of the Brailack, stopping him in his tracks. Gabe stands. "There is a portable airlock aboard the *Ghost*." He heads back towards the Ankarran Raptor.

Wil looks around. "So..."

Maxim moves to examine some of the cargo crates. "Len, you've mentioned several times that you know who lives here. Who is it?"

The research droid turns. "This station was used by Farsight to house the experiments that were deemed a success, at least until they were moved to other facilities. There were several..." The droid pauses, somehow, in vacuum, and without a face in the biological sense, showing the pain the retelling of this story brings it. "...Specimens that were more or less permanent residents of the station."

"So, not just one person?" Maxim asks.

"How can you be sure he, they, it, is still here?" Zephyr asks.

"Excuse me." Gabe steps between them toward the stuck airlock hatch. He sets about assembling a framework around the hatch. As the frame takes form, thin membranes stretch between the sections.

Len continues, "While I cannot be one hundred percent certain, I believe that when this station was closed down, those in charge would have left the test subjects here to die. They were, after all, test subjects. Others could be created. Transporting them could have opened them to additional risk."

"Dark," Bennie says. Len nods slowly.

"The temporary airlock is complete," Gabe says, standing. He holds an arm out, beckoning the others to enter. The temporary airlock is nothing more than a metal frame with transparent polymer stretched over the frame. It is four meters long and three wide, more than enough room for everyone to enter at once. Gabe and Maxim force the busted airlock doors apart. They don't try to slide closed.

Once inside the station proper, Wil has Jarvis send the ducklings and Launchpad off to map out the station. Len was able to provide a basic idea of the layout before they arrived. Wil points down a dark corridor. "Okay, we've successfully entered the scary haunted space station portion of the job."

"Haven't we done this already?" Bennie quips, walking past Wil, his hand on the hilt of his beam saber. C7K2 had helped Bennie construct his own device a few months after the funeral for Sir Jarek Ruus. Bennie's blade is bright blue, the hilt sized to his small hands.

"Yeah, and the same monsters are waiting at the end," Maxim quips.

Bennie releases his beam saber from the clip on his belt. "Yay."

# WARM WELCOME_

"So where is your 'maybe here, maybe not here' friend likely to be?" Wil asks as they pass through a cafeteria. Chairs and tables are tipped over and litter the space. On his wristcomm, four small icons are moving about an ever increasingly detailed wireframe of the station.

Bennie opens a cupboard, the lights on his shoulders illuminating the interior. "Pretty picked over."

Len is looking around. "The residential—"

"I am detecting movement," Gabe interrupts.

The cafeteria gets a little brighter, followed by the snap hiss of Bennie's beam saber.

"Help me, Obi-Wan..." Wil whispers under his breath.

Bennie makes a rude gesture. "My hearing is better than yours. We've been over this." Wil smiles.

Cynthia has a pulse pistol in each hand. She moves to stand next to Wil. "Where?" she asks.

Gabe points to a hatch opposite the one they came through. His eyes are red. He is pointing with an arm blaster. Maxim moves to the hatch, hand on the manual release. Gabe raises his other arm, nodding. Maxim pulls the release and pulls the hatch in.

Nothing.

Gabe strides forward through the hatch arms moving to form a T. As he turns to face the others, a solid mass erupts from the ceiling in the cafeteria, landing in between Wil and Zephyr. Ceiling tiles fly everywhere. A powerful arm lashes out to send Wil hurtling across the room to crash into a chair. Zephyr spins, her rifle whining as super charged plasma erupts from the muzzle. Several bolts strike the dark shape before it moves to put Cynthia between it and Zephyr.

Maxim rushes towards them, only to be tripped by a chair kicked at his feet. Cynthia spins, firing both of her pistols. Several more bolts strike the thing. It makes no sound. Gabe rushes back in, leaping over Maxim, firing as he flies through the air. The creature uses a chair to deflect most of the energy bolts, then hurtles the chair at the droid.

Bennie moves fast, faster than the others, except maybe Maxim, have seen him move before. His blue blade whirs as it slices through the air to impact and cut into a chitin-covered arm.

"Ouch!" the thing shouts, kicking Bennie in the chest, sending him flying further than Wil did.

The ink black creature that speaks galactic standard darts out the hatch the team entered the cafeteria through, vanishing.

Wil looks around, his shoulder lights washing over the others. "Ouch?" He turns to Len. "Your friend?"

The droid tilts their head. "'Friend' is not quite the correct term, but yes, that was Jacoby."

"Jacoby?" Bennie repeats rubbing his armored chest. He clips his beam saber to the hook on his armor's hip. "What's the deal?" He turns to Len.

The droid looks around. "Jacoby was—is—a Multonae man who worked in Farsight research. They transferred him to the Source Project because of his lack of surviving family. He was experimented on, ultimately being treated with DNA from the...you called them Monster C. The DNA treatments culminated in the changes you saw." They turn to Bennie. "Do not worry about his limb. It will regrow."

"Limb regrowth? They couldn't do that," Cynthia says.

Maxim nods. "Thank the gods." Zephyr nods her agreement, shuddering.

Len inclines their head again. "It was a side effect, an interaction with Multonae and Source DNA. Not all subjects experienced it."

"Imagine an army of Rhys Duch's that can regrow limbs."

Wil huffs. "The entire race isn't stupid, right?"

Bennie makes a face. "Humans are." Wil flips him off.

"Don't forget, they also end up looking like Gunji beetles," Zephyr points out.

Cynthia shudders. "Yeah, even in the dark, that thing was kinda nightmarish."

Len looks at the hatch Jacoby fled through. "We should attempt to follow. I suspect his attack was his normal reaction to invaders. If I can get his attention, he may let us explain our visit."

"May?" Wil presses.

The droid makes a shrugging motion.

"It also avoided your probes," Maxim points out.

Wil shudders.

"So, this bug-guy, Jacoby? He's lived here, what? A year now, alone?" Bennie says from the middle of the single file line they're walking in. The station's main corridor runs from the hangar to the reactor complex, smaller corridors branching off every fifty meters or so.

Len looks back. "Yes. As I understand it, this station was decommissioned approximately a cycle ago." They pass a section of wall that has been ripped apart and re-wired. "Farsight pulled out, likely enacting their housecleaning protocol. Jacoby seems to have worked fast to save himself and the others."

"You mentioned others before," Maxim says.

They turn down a side corridor. Len says, "During my time aboard the station, there were twelve...residents."

"Twelve monsters like that guy?" Cynthia asks.

"No. Each of the long-term residents was different. This facility focused on the interactions of Source DNA with that of GC races." Len leads them down another corridor. "Farsight was attempting to find out which races would be most compatible and result in the fewest mutations."

"Pleasant thought," Zephyr says.

"They ultimately found that there were no mutation-free combinations." Len pushes a hatch open. They're knocked backwards, toppling into Maxim. The two go down in a pile of limbs and cursing.

The remaining crew focus their armor lights and weapons on the hatch. Standing in it is a nearly three-meter-tall, chitin-armored monster with a vaguely humanoid face, except for the eyes and segmented mandible-like jaw. Like the skeletal, elongated skulls of the Monster C's, Jacoby's eye sockets are empty and covered in the same ink black chitin.

"Who the grolack are you?" the mutant Multonae croaks.

Wil helps Maxim up off Len. "Jacoby?"

The big man-creature looks at Wil, then the others. His eyeless face settles on Bennie. He makes a growl-like clicking sound.

Bennie holds both hands up. "Hey, man, sorry about, you know... your arm."

Jacoby grunts, a second set of arms unfolding from around his torso. "I have extras."

Len regains their feet. "Hello, Jacoby."

The creature steps out into the corridor, head tilted. "I know you?"

"I was assigned here a cycle ago. I was one of the researchers," Len says.

Jacoby growls again. This time the clicking sound is like angry bees.

Zephyr steps forward. "We need your help."

"My help?"

Once everyone is calm, Jacoby escorts them further aft, toward the reactor complex and secure lab facilities. "Farsight gave the residents pretty free rein here, so when they started discreetly packing up, we noticed," he says, pushing aside a piece of wall paneling to reveal a makeshift corridor where none is meant to be. "Wlen was the first to notice. She told the rest of us. We got to work."

He looks over his shoulder as the group files in behind him. "They didn't know we knew about the housecleaning protocol."

"Why didn't you just fight back?" Maxim asks. "From what we've seen, you're a capable fighter."

The ink black head bows. "I am, but most of the others aren't. Multonae DNA is..." He holds out the arm Bennie cut the forearm off of. A new limb is already visible, soft and pink, sticking out of the stump. "...Compatible to a high degree. Other GC races aren't nearly as fortunate."

"Fortunate?" Cynthia asks.

"You'll see," the big man says. "We're here." He pushes aside another panel. It screeches as it slides across the metal deck. Several heads of various sizes and configuration turn to look at the new arrivals.

"Holy shit," Wil whispers.

## MISFIT TOYS_

Jacoby raises an arm. "It's fine. They're not a threat."

A creature waddles over on short, stumpy legs from a low table it had been working at. It's shorter than Bennie, not by much. Like Jacoby, the eyes have vanished, but this creature has fleshy sockets. Its mouth seems to span the width of the head, a head with fleshy shoulder-length, dreadlock-like tentacles sprouting from it. "I'm Wlen."

Bennie eyes the hybrid. "Brailack?"

"Once upon a time. I was a junior research assistant in the starship R&D division. I caught a senior executive doing something he wasn't supposed to be doing, and when I reported it, was assigned here." She holds out an arm that still looks like flesh, but with black scales here and there. "My reward."

Bennie looks up at his friends. "This is wrong. Farsight falsified their records so that the commission wouldn't even know this place was here. Even thinking they'd cleaned house and the most anyone would find would be bodies, they still hid this place." He shudders.

Cynthia kneels down. "We'll make sure everyone knows."

"No," another being says, moving to join them. "We don't want people to know about us. To see us, like this." She has a vaguely humanoid physique; her arms are twice as long as one would expect, nearly dragging on the floor. They end in long, bone thin fingers. Three of them and two thumbs. Her elongated skull has ridges running along its top. Zephyr takes a sharp breath. She approaches the woman. "Palorian?"

The woman nods. "Breeze. I was a security officer here." Her skin is more chitin than not, but not like Jacoby's, not a carapace. "No one needs to see this." She raises an arm, letting a thin, fleshy membrane unfold, revealing that her arms are bat-like wings. "We're monsters. Failed experiments. I don't want anyone to see me like this. To know of my weakness."

Zephyr rests a hand on the deformed woman's shoulder. "You survived the experiments and this. Weakness is not something I would ascribe to you." She gestures to the others. "To any of you."

Jacoby turns to Len, then Wil. "You mentioned needing my," he looks around, "*our* help."

Wil outlines the job in broad brushstrokes: stolen data, data that could let criminal organizations continue Farsight's nightmare programs. The likely whereabouts of the data and difficulty in getting to it.

Jacoby nods as he hears the explanation. When Wil finishes, he says, "I think we can help you, in exchange for your help."

"Name it," Wil replies.

"You take all of us, and when we're done, we don't come back here."

One of the small painted spheres appears, zipping around the ceiling of the communal living space. Several of the hybrids crouch. Jacoby turns to Wil, making a hissing noise.

Wil raises both hands. "Sorry, just a sensor drone." He watches the drone move around. It's Huey. "A drone with really poor timing," he says louder.

From the speaker in his helmet, Jarvis says, "Sorry, sir."

# CHAPTER 9_

## YOU THOUGHT THIS WOULD
## BE EASY_

"Sir, I believe we have a problem," Jarvis says. Another sensor drone has zipped into the cavernous space. This time the hybrids don't flinch. It is painted burnt orange, Launchpad.

"What's up?" Wil looks around. Several of the hybrids are gathering their scant belongings. Jacoby and Wlen are directing them.

"Dewey is detecting an instability in the gravity systems of this station. It appears our landing in the hangar has thrown things out of whack."

"Out of whack?"

"I have been studying your media archives while the armor is in storage," the AI explains. "The added mass of the *Ghost* seems to have affected the station in unexpected ways."

"Sounds bad," Wil says. He motions Gabe over, tapping an icon on his wristcomm to bridge Jarvis into the team comms. "Repeat your last, Jarvis."

"Hello, Gabe. I was explaining to the Captain that our landing in the hangar has caused an instability within the station's gravity systems."

"That is not good," Gabe replies.

"Indeed. From the readings I am getting from Dewey, the reactor was already likely unstable, but the additional mass of the *Ghost* within the hangar has stressed the system beyond its ability to compensate."

"We must attempt repairs," Gabe says.

"I am opening a data link," Jarvis says. Wil looks around, watching the others help the hybrids prepare. He makes eye contact, he thinks, with Jacoby and waves him over.

Gabe turns to Wil. "Captain, we must hurry. The reactor is already in the early stages of meltdown."

"Meltdown?" Jacoby repeats. "What are you talking about?"

Wil turns to the insectoid-looking man. "Looks like our landing in the hangar started a chain reaction, for lack of a better term. The gravity systems were failing, and when we landed, it pushed them too far. Your reactor is failing."

Gabe says, "We must hurry."

Jacoby raises a hand, the hand Bennie had cut off, now almost fully regrown, hardened chitin still wet looking. "T'Kinlo is in the engineering section. We must get to her."

"Who?" Wil asks.

"She was an engineer, *is* an engineer. She's been keeping this place running. She either knows the reactor is in trouble and is already trying or does not realize the danger."

Gabe says, "There is nothing to stop the failure. If she is trying, she is wasting her time."

Wil looks around, "Bennie, you and Zee take Jacoby and go get the engineer. We'll get everyone else to the *Ghost*."

Bennie nods and looks across the room to Zephyr, who returns the nod. The Brailack turns to Jacoby. "Come on, big guy. Let's go get your friend." He turns and looks around. "Door?" Jacoby makes a noise and gestures to a piece of metal leaning against a wall.

"So, what's the deal?" Jacoby asks as he leads Zephyr and Bennie further aft. The station shudders. "That's new." The vibration lasts only a few seconds.

Bennie looks around. "How much further?"

"Couple hundred meters," Jacoby replies, increasing his pace.

Zephyr looks up at the insect-featured man. "They didn't even tell you, did they?"

Jacoby looks down, frowning. "Not a peep. For just over two cycles, Farsight tinkered with that monster DNA. When things didn't work, they ended up here to be destroyed. When things worked," he rests an armored black hand against his chest, "they studied them." He makes a clicking growl sound. "Farsight security made a habit of snatching people who asked too many questions or simply had no one who would ask about them."

Bennie sighs. "We thought Asgar was a good guy."

Zephyr nods. "Yeah, we really called that one wrong." Bennie's head bobs aggressively.

Jacoby grunts. "Before joining Farsight, I worked for a company on Multonae doing research. I thought the gig with Farsight was a dream come true." His second set of arms unfolds, and he holds all four hands out. "It's a nightmare."

# YOU'D BE WRONG_

Zephyr stops the trio in the corridor. "I'm so sorry."

Jacoby's eyeless face turns to her. The way he turns to her is like the monsters on Glacial did, knowing exactly where to look even without eyes. "You didn't cause this. You didn't make Asgar the monster he is—"

"Was," Bennie interrupts. Jacoby turns to the small Brailack, who coughs awkwardly. "We're the reason Farsight collapsed. Asgar is dead."

"Really?" The insect-featured man can't hide his surprise. "I—we just assumed they abandoned this place because they got something better."

"Gods, I hope not," Zephyr exhales.

"This way." Jacoby resumes walking. Something somewhere groans and something somewhere else nearby breaks and makes a clanging sound that echoes.

The engineering space of the station isn't as big as Zephyr expects. Based on the rest of the station, it is exactly as decrepit and dirty as she expects.

"These the drennogs that grolacked us?" someone shouts from somewhere near the top of the number two reactor. Something about two meters long, covered in green and black oversized scales, scurries down to the deck. "You trying to kill us?" the used-to-be-Trenbal woman demands. She grimaces as several fleshy tentacles wriggle from under her enlarged scales.

Zephyr steps forward. "We're not trying to kill you, and we are sorry our arrival messed up your station. We need—"

"I'll fix it. I always do." T'Kinlo turns away.

Jacoby stops her. "Tee, we have to go."

The woman spins, her tail dragging across the deck. Spines that aren't typical for Trenbal leave slight scratches in the deck's metal. "What the wurrin do you mean?"

Reactor one shakes on its mounting bracket. Jacoby points. "According to their droid, there's nothing you can do."

"Like wurrin, I can't!" she growls, moving toward the still shaking reactor.

"You can't!" Bennie shouts. "This place is done. You gotta come with us! Now!" He watches as a piece of wall panel falls, clattering to the deck. "Don't be dumb."

The Trenbal turns. "Dumb? I was second team engineering lead for this station."

Bennie holds up a hand. "And now you're a freaky monster because Farsight is evil. We've—" He stops speaking because a pair of green, black scaled hands wraps around his throat.

"Woah!" Jacoby and Zephyr shout in unison. Both of them reach for the angry engineer, prying her hands off Bennie.

Jacoby sighs loudly. "Tee, we have to go. For better or worse, their arrival was the last straw for this place." Another wall panel falls to the ground. "We have to go."

The engineer looks around the cavernous space. She takes a deep breath and exhales. "Fine." She looks at Bennie. "I might still choke you later."

Bennie rasps, "As long as it's aboard the *Ghost*." He turns and motions for everyone to leave, turning to look the Trenbal engineer up and down.

Zephyr falls in next to him. "Feeling okay?"

Bennie rubs his neck. "Yeah, why?"

She shrugs. "You're a little more surly than normal."

He makes a rude gesture. "I don't know how the Knights did it."

"With practice." Zephyr smiles.

"How do you have so much stuff?" Wil asks one of the hybrids, a being that he thinks was a Sylban, the tree-like race he's encountered here and there. The creature, normally just over two meters tall, is now closer to three. His bark-like skin is dotted with four-centimeter-long thorns that slip through gaps in bark-like skin that's now a mixture of bark and chitin. He, too, is eyeless. *Shitty side effect*, Wil thinks to himself. The station shudders, causing several of the hybrids to stumble.

The creature reaches for a conduit overhead. He opens his mouth, but no sound comes out. He closes his mouth and looks at Wil, then opens it again. Still no sound.

When the Sylban man stares at him without moving, Wil looks around. "Little help here?"

Wlen comes over. "Sekma doesn't speak. He can't—the mutation took his voice." She looks up at the man towering over her and Wil. She makes a few hand gestures. Sekma nods and walks over to join the other hybrids.

Wil looks at her. "Space sign language, cool." She makes a face, her confusion obvious. From across the room, Wil hears Cynthia sigh and say something about *telling Zephyr*.

ALWAYS SOMETHING_

It turns out that while there may have been almost a dozen original residents, not all of them have survived the year stranded on the derelict station. Twice, pirates have stumbled onto the station and boarded it. Both times the invaders were repelled, at a cost. The station shudders, and this time it doesn't stop. The few functional light panels stutter.

"Gonna be crowded," Wil says, looking around the corridor. Several pieces of wall panel clatter to the deck. The crew of the *Ghost* and remaining residents of Meltrom station are standing in the corridor outside the hangar. "The *Ghost* doesn't have a lot of spare guest beds. We'll figure it out, though." He looks around. "I don't suppose you all have space suits?"

Jacoby chuckles. "We don't need them." He's holding one of their group, a creature that used to be an Olop woman but now resembles a cross between a nearly three-meter-long sea turtle and a llama. Demfley her name is. Her hands have become flippers and under the hair that covers her body, black scales have formed. Her legs have shrunk to nearly useless stumps. According to Jacoby, the bulk of what is under the shell is an air bladder that can be compressed and released from biological maneuvering thrusters in her hands and feet.

"One consistent side effect of the hybridization is that we can go long periods of time in vacuum."

"Handy," Maxim says.

Wil steps into the airlock. "Okay, follow us, then." He motions the crew into the temporary airlock Gabe constructed earlier. As his helmet seals up, he looks at Len. "Even if they can't help, I'm glad you brought us here." The droid inclines their head. Wil looks to Gabe, who mimics the gesture.

As they walk from the airlock to the ship, Wil looks back to see the motley crew of hybrids following behind, all sans spacesuit. Demfley is drifting along next to the group, small jets of air guiding her along. Several of her friends are clinging to her shell. "That's pretty cool."

Cynthia turns to follow Wil's gaze. "You don't like going to the bathroom at restaurants..."

He blushes as he hears Bennie's snicker over the comms. "What's that got to—"

"Where do you think she goes?"

"Oh..."

"Yeah."

Maxim looks back to watch the hybrids. "It's impressive how the Source DNA expresses so differently when mixed with other DNA." He points to Jacoby, who is also anchoring several other hybrids. His powerful toes and the claws extended from them are gouging the deck plating enough to give him purchase in the low gravity of the hangar. The others are clinging to various parts of his chitinous hide.

Once the thick cargo bay doors clang shut, everyone removes their helmets. Wil looks at the assorted hybrids, the smallest just shorter than Bennie, and the largest nearly half a meter taller than Maxim. "So, we've got two guest berths, which are both double bunks, but..."

"We can sleep down here," Jacoby offers. "We've gotten used to fewer...creature comforts." He's holding Demfley again, her mutation making living in space easy, living under the influence of gravity, less so. He gently sets her down off to the side.

Wil nods and looks at his crew. "Okay, let's get out of our armor. I'll get us moving and you all can get our friends situated." He looks around, noticing that Len is still standing near the cargo doors, well away from everyone. He nods to the shy droid.

As the crew of the *Ghost* walks along the neck toward the bridge and the armory below it, the ship shakes, thanks to the station she's sitting in shaking itself apart. Wil looks at the others. "I'll get us underway. I don't like the feel of this." He motions to everything outside the *Ghost*. The others nod and take the port and starboard stairs down to the armory to change out of their gear.

Wil drops into his command seat. Flipping switches to bring the ship out of standby, he looks around at the empty stations. "Just like old times," he whispers as the familiar rumble of the reactor coming up to power vibrates the deck. When the power level indicator turns green, he looks at the primary display as he pushes the power lever for the repulsor lifts forward, easing power levels up. The *Ghost* lifts off the deck, her powerful landing gear folding up underneath her.

On the screen, the station's hangar shifts. Wil looks at his console to ensure he isn't messing something up. An indicator light starts blinking. "Oh, shit." He reaches for the sub-light engine throttle, pushing it forward sharply.

"This is certainly different," Maxim says, pulling the chest piece of his armor over his head. Zephyr takes it, placing it on a hook in Maxim's alcove. He continues, "So, we know more or less where to go. Now we have a small army of misfits tagging along. How does this get us closer to our goal?"

The rumble of the reactor vibrates the deck. Everyone looks up at a small display that shows the ship's status. The reactor is powering up.

Cynthia slips out of her armor undergarment, reaching for her shipboard jumpsuit. "I actually have some thoughts on that," she says. She reaches down for her boots. "Wil has told me the story of your trip to the Barsoom system enough times that I think I can recite every detail, from every point of view."

The deck shifts under their feet as the *Ghost* lifts off the deck of the soon-to-be destroyed station. They're forced to grab the edges of their armor storage areas. "All this time and he's still not very good at take offs," Bennie grouses. He stands up, pulling his own diminutive armor chest piece over his head just as the ship lurches. Bennie flies across the small armory, screeching.

Maxim grips the edge of his armory alcove, holding Zephyr's elbow as the ship tilts, the g forces pushing them aft.

Over the ceiling speaker, Wil says, "Sorry."

# ABSOLUTION ISN'T EASY_

Cᴙɴᴛʜɪᴀ sᴛᴇᴘs ᴏᴜᴛ of the small refresher in the berth she and Wil share, a towel wrapped around her, another in her hands, ruffling the fur on her face, her tail swishing languidly. "I wonder if the training modules Zarrix loaded you up with way back need a refresher?"

Wil is sitting on the bed, one boot on. "I don't need flight training."

"Bennie's forehead might disagree," she replies, dropping her towel and reaching for the jumpsuit she put on in the armory.

"Okay, creeper. I can feel your eye," she says playfully.

"Just admiring the view," Wil says, smiling. "Why do you think Len had us come out here?"

"I think they saw it as a chance to help these people. Maybe help us?" she replies, now fully dressed. "Come on." She presses the release on the hatch to their berth.

Wil rubs his face. "Intriguing."

Mᴀxɪᴍ, Zᴇᴘʜʏʀ, ᴀɴᴅ Bᴇɴɴɪᴇ ᴀʀᴇ ɪɴ ᴛʜᴇ ᴄᴀʀɢᴏ ʜᴏʟᴅ ᴡɪᴛʜ the hybrids. Bennie is handing out snacks while the two Palorians hand out bulbs of water. Occasionally, the team hacker stops to rub a sizable knot on his head.

Maxim approaches Breeze, the hybrid that used to be a Palorian woman. "How are you doing?"

She takes the water bulb between fingers almost as long as Maxim's forearm. "I thought I'd die on that station." She looks around. "So this is an improvement, minor that it is."

Maxim chuckles. "Is there anyone we should try to reach on your behalf?"

The woman makes a noise somewhere between a laugh and a screech. "How would that work? *Your daughter isn't dead after all. She's a horribly disfigured monster that can turn invisible.*"

Maxim arches an eyebrow. "Invisible?"

The Palorian hybrid nods. As she speaks, she fades from view as if she's losing cohesion. Her bulb of water seemingly floating in midair. "Something in the Source DNA allows me to absorb light." She returns to normal. "It's exhausting, but it was handy before Farsight pulled out."

"Does Wlen have that ability? Is that how she found out they were going to kill you all?" Maxim catches Bennie's eye and motions him over. When the Brailack arrives, Maxim says, "You got your tablet?" Bennie nods. "Start an inventory."

"Inventory of what?" the hacker replies.

Before Maxim can answer, Breeze answers his earlier question. "No, Wlen can..." She searches for the right words. "...Change her size? I guess is how you'd describe it."

Bennie's hairless brow ridges rise. "Like the main Source baddy?"

Maxim nods. "That would be my guess." He looks around the cargo hold at the assorted beings then turns back to Breeze. "On top of your physical changes, I'm guessing you all picked up...abilities?"

She nods. "Most of us, yes." She sighs. "The Farsight teams were attempting to harness the abilities without the physical mutations." She shakes her head once. "They were unsuccessful."

Maxim and Bennie exchange a look before the Brailack heads off to talk with another hybrid, someone that looks like a spider with a fleshy, toothless mouth and large, chitinous thorax. If Maxim remembers correctly, it was a Malkorite man.

T'Kinlo sidles up next to Maxim. "So, what's up? Why did you all come to the station?"

Maxim tilts his head. "Len."

"The researcher?" the Trenbal engineer asks.

"The same. He suggested we come here, that you all might be able to help us."

"With?"

From where he's standing next to the arachnid hybrid, Bennie grins. "Crime."

Maxim tuts. "Sanctioned crime."

IN ENGINEERING, GABE AND LEN ARE STANDING PERFECTLY still.

"You should be proud. Those people would have died on that station had you not brought us," Gabe says.

"Helping them was not something I had thought I would be able to do. It feels good. I do not believe it voids my earlier bad acts, but—" the gray droid says but is cut off.

"You cannot erase past actions." Gabe tilts his head. "You can only endeavor to be better moving forward."

Len nods. "I hope I am able to."

"You are off to a good start," the engineer says, then adds, "You knew of their abilities."

The research droid nods again. "I did. When you told me of your reason for coming to me, that the archives were stolen and where they were most likely being kept, it occurred to me that these people and their skills might be of use." When Gabe does not immediately answer, Len adds, "Can I go home now?"

Gabe busies himself with the reactor control panel. "Is your plan to remain on Arcadia, in a basement forever?" He turns to the other droid. "Why not simply shut down?"

Len moves to the recharging station Gabe has fitted into a small alcove. Since moving his spark to his new body, Gabe no longer needs to charge. The power cell in the Amalgamation of Parts body design he chose is exceptionally efficient. Len turns to Gabe. "I do not know. I know I did horrible things to those people." The thin metallic arm gestures in the direction of the cargo hold below. "Saving them has helped ease my conscience, but it is not absolution."

"Will absolution come while you hide in a basement?"

The *Ghost* continues away from the star and the rapidly expanding debris cloud that was Meltrom station.

# PART THREE

# CHAPTER 10_

# BACK TO SCHOOL_

"WE WERE BEGINNING to think you had taken the deposit and run off," Mress says from the primary display. Her eyes move to take in the bridge of the *Ghost*. They stop on Jacoby, who's standing at the bridge hatch. "Hello."

Jacoby inclines his eyeless head. "Hello."

Wil looks over his shoulder. "Long story. Chock one more in the *Farsight were evil dicks* column. This is Jacoby. He and his friends are with us on this, and they're gonna need someplace to live when we're done."

"I...see," she says.

Zephyr looks at Wil, then the primary display. "You mentioned having assets we could use if we figured out where the data arcs are being kept. We're reasonably certain that we have."

"You have?" Mress asks.

"More or less," Zephyr amends.

Bennie rubs his forehead. "Sorta."

Mress looks at the Brailack, then Wil. "Sorta?"

Wil coughs. "We're pretty sure we know where the arcs are, but we can't be sure on our own."

"I see." The elder Tygran woman looks off to the side and nods.

She turns back. "I'm transmitting coordinates. Call me when you arrive." She smiles, and the screen goes black.

"Sending the coordinates to your station," Cynthia says.

Wil nods. "Got 'em. Looks like a couple days FTL." The stars on the main display shift as the *Ghost* adjusts her course. A minute later, the stars stretch out into the familiar streaks of FTL. He looks over his shoulder to Jacoby. "You like tacos?"

The previously Multonae man looks around the bridge, his gaze settling on Maxim. "Tah-kose?"

Wil stands. "I'll get started."

Bennie says, "I'll help." He glares at Wil, rubbing his forehead. "I have a few things to shout at you about."

Maxim stands and rests a hand on the big bug-like man's shoulder. "You or any of your friends have dietary restrictions?"

Jacoby grunts. "Sekma doesn't have teeth."

"Soft tacos it is," Cynthia says, putting her station into standby.

Jacoby passes through the common deck, heading for the staircase down to the cargo hold. "I'll let the others know to get ready for dinner." He nods to Wil as he closes the hatch.

Bennie is grating klorm, which is as close to cheese as Wil has found. The Brailack looks up. "I think we should look at the programming on your neural upgrade."

"I think you can choke on a bag of di—" A handful of klorm strikes him in the face.

Bennie points to his forehead and the dark lump still there. "I'm serious."

Wil makes a noise and stirs the ground jerlack he's seasoning. "Fine."

"Just for takeoffs," Bennie offers, trying to make his human friend feel better. "And maybe landings? Have you had it looked at since it was installed?"

Wil brandishes a blunt utensil he uses to break up the frozen ground meat. "Go help someone else." Bennie shrugs and walks away.

As Bennie enters the staircase that connects all the decks of the *Ghost*, Cynthia and Zephyr come out. The two women exchange words with Bennie, then look at Wil. "We're supposed to say supportive things about you being open to running your neural implant upgrade through some diagnostics," Zephyr says.

Cynthia adds, "I suggested it and you got pissy. Little green brings it up and you're open to it?" She looks at Zephyr. "Maybe he only listens to people with laser swords?"

Wil turns. "I'm not sharing my hot sauce with you."

Zephyr makes a face. "Didn't need to hear that."

Wil's cheeks burn a deep crimson. "Not that!" He looks at Cynthia. "You can always—"

"Nope!" Cynthia shouts and grabs a stack of plates and a fistful of utensils. She says nothing further as she nudges the hatch to the staircase open and leaves.

Zephyr and Wil exchange an awkward glance as she grabs supplies and bottles of water for everyone.

# WHITE RABBIT_

"These are delicious," Breeze says. She's got half of a taco grasped between two of her long, delicate fingers. She uses them like chopsticks.

The crew and the hybrids are gathered in the cargo hold around a makeshift community table. Someone assembled it from pieces of wall panel and small crates and sat it on the sparring mat so that everyone could sit on the ground comfortably.

"Agreed! Where did you say your planet was? They have these there?" Demfley says. While Wil and the crew were getting underway and making dinner, Gabe gave the used-to-be-an-Olop woman a modified grav sled to get around on. She's hovering near the head of the table.

Wil smiles. "I mean, they don't grow on trees or anything, but yeah, tacos are pretty ubiquitous." He looks around the cargo hold, smiling at the assorted mutated beings sitting, standing, hovering near the table. Crew members of the *Ghost* are mixed throughout the group, chatting with their guests.

Wil looks at Jacoby. "So they just left ya? How come you guys didn't stop them or take over a shuttle and leave them on the station?"

Jacoby finishes chewing a bit of taco and turns his eyeless face to

Wil. He doesn't say anything, instead turning to T'Kinlo. "Tee, want to explain why we didn't stop the Farsight scientists from leaving?"

The Trenbal woman grunts, rising to her feet. "Easier to show you." She walks towards the spider-like creature. Wil recalls his name being Bol Kar, a Malkorite. Now the man is a daddy long legs with fanlike ears and a pulsing chitinous and semitransparent thorax. Bol Kar shifts to reveal his underside to T'Kinlo.

She points to the spider-like thorax with pulsing organs shifting inside. Her clawed fingertip points to something with a blinking light. "Bomb." She turns to Wil and the others. "We all have one. Every member of the science team had the ability to kill any or all of us."

"Why didn't they?" Maxim asks as T'Kinlo moves back to her spot at the table.

Jacoby takes over to answer. "They felt they were doing us a kindness. The station was well stocked. The station administrator said that Farsight would be forging documents to make it seem the station was long ago decommissioned to keep people away." He makes a clicking, growling noise. "They said we'd be safe. Said they'd send supplies from time to time."

"They didn't consider pirates," Wlen offers, her head tentacles twitching.

"Or live up to the whole 'sending of supplies' thing," Jacoby adds.

Zephyr nods, her face grim. "How many?"

Wlen shoves a taco into her wide set mouth. Jacoby answers, "There were nearly two tens of us." He sighs. "Twice pirates and salvagers came to the station. The first time we met them, hoping they'd trade, or better yet, take us with them. They killed the welcoming party." He puts one of his larger hands on a section of his chitinous torso. "Most of the welcoming party. I survived."

Wlen finishes chewing. "The next group didn't have the benefit of our naivete." Her face is grim.

Bol Kar chimes in, "Unfortunately, both times the invaders were able to keep us from gaining access to their ships."

"Bummer," Wil mumbles. Several heads nod.

Cynthia, sitting next to Wil, finishes her taco. "Okay, this is solemn. How about a movie?" She turns to Gabe and Len, standing silently off to the side, "Gabe, can we rig up a projection device?"

Len raises a hand. "I have the ability to holo-project." They turn to the aft bulkhead, and as a section of their torso shifts and opens, a three-by-five-meter flat, white rectangle appears. Len turns their head. "I do not have access to your media archive." Gabe extends a hand, data tendrils snacking out of his fingertips. After a few seconds, they retract. Len inclines their head. "Thank you." They turn to Cynthia. "What would you like to watch?"

Cynthia looks around the room, smiling. "How about the one where everyone is inside a simulation?"

Wil nods. "*The Matrix*. Solid choice. We have time for all six." He nods to Len.

## INCOMING_

`"So, any of you ever been here before?" Wil asks as the stretched-out star lines of FTL shrink back to pinpricks of light. In the distance, on the primary display, one of the pinpricks is a little bigger and brighter than the others, and growing.

Zephyr looks up from her console. "A few times. Kobona is a mid-tier system. Kobona Four is a colony, actually. No natives."

Maxim adds, "All domes. I hate dome planets."

Cynthia chuckles. "I was here once, for a job."

Bennie turns around. "Like a stab, stab, kill, kill job or just an errand for Zarrix?"

Cynthia tilts her head to the side, flashing her teeth. "Guess."

Wil shudders. "Great. Well, at least you guys know the terrain." He turns to Maxim. "Domes?"

Zephyr answers for him. "Kobona Four's orbit is just outside the habitable zone. Frozen surface, subterranean oceans." She consults her console. "Despite that, they've done well for themselves, highly industrialized. The ocean is full of life and valuable minerals."

"Whose colony is it?" Wil wonders.

Zephyr consults her screen again. "Good question." She taps a few keys. "I thought so. It's a GC colony, one of the old open emigration colonies from the expansion effort."

The bridge hatch opens, and Jacoby and Wlen enter, the latter clinging to the former's chitinous carapace. The smaller hybrid looks at the screen. The Kobona system primary is now clearly visible. "So, this is the Kobona system."

Wil nods as he looks over his shoulder. "Yeah. I was about to call our contact and figure out next steps."

"We'll leave you to it," Jacoby says, turning to the hatch.

"Stay." Wil smiles. "At least for now, you're crew and you're part of this."

"We get paid?" the used-to-be-Brailack woman asks.

Wil looks at Bennie. "Cultural thing?" The hacker makes a rude gesture. He turns to Jacoby and Wlen. "No."

"I've got Miss Mress," Cynthia announces.

A window on the primary display appears with the seal of the Galactic Commonwealth. A bland musical tune fills the bridge.

Wil looks over his shoulder at his girlfriend, who shrugs. "I guess we're on hold." On the larger portion of the main display, the star Kobona continues to increase in size.

A minute later the music abruptly stops, and everyone on the bridge looks at the primary display. Barbara Mress and Selmak are on the screen. The Tarsi woman nods. "Sorry, we were making arrangements for you to meet with our assets planet-side."

Wil nods. "No worries. Catchy hold muzak." The two women on screen exchange a look, so Wil presses on. "So, we're here, Kobona Four, or will be in another hour or so. What's the deal?"

Barbara nods. "That timing should work. We've arranged for a meeting between you and the team lead in three tocks. I'm transmitting the details, but the high-level overview is that the Governing Council has a small cadre of operators that it uses for sensitive missions. Things that are better not being done by the Peacekeepers. Things that are better kept off of official records."

"Black ops, cool," Wil says, nodding along.

"This team is currently on Kobona Four. The team lead, Nellin, will meet you."

"What job are they doing?" Zephyr asks.

"Infiltrating the Consortium," Selmak replies matter-of-factly.

Maxim leans forward. "If you've got agents in the Consortium, what are we doing?"

"The Consortium is here? On Kobona?" Bennie asks.

Barbara clears her throat. "You're doing what they can't. Shadow Six—"

"Cool name," Wil interrupts.

Mress sighs. "Shadow Six has been working for more than a cycle on infiltrating the Consortium. Two of the team vanished within the span of ten days, presumably their covers blown. Two more are currently holding low-level positions."

Maxim holds up his hand to re-ask his question, but Mress continues, "Unfortunately, the Consortium is intensely secretive and multi-layered. Our operatives are so lowly placed they have yet to even confirm it was the Consortium who stole the data arcs."

"Sounds useful," Cynthia quips.

On the main display, the star Kobona is growing larger and larger. The computer is highlighting planets, moons, and other interesting bodies as they become visible.

Selmak bows her head. "Indeed. However, we believe that one of them is uniquely placed to help you now that you know where the arcs are likely being kept."

## UNWANTED VISITORS_

"How was Epsilon Eridani?" Wil asks. He's in his quarters. The rest of the crew is watching an episode of *The X-Files* reboot, one of the later season's episodes. Wil keeps Greenwich Mean Time in a widget on his wristcomm, so he can remember when to chat with James. It should be just after dinner, ship time, for his friend.

"Good. We're almost home. Man, I see why you didn't come back. This is so damn awesome." He gestures at something beyond the range of the camera. "I've been to another star system. Ten freakin' light years from Earth."

Wil grins. "I told you. Way back at the Costco. You thought I was being melodramatic."

James nods. "I'd be lying if I said I hadn't thought about giving the order to set a course for..." He rubs his chin. "I have no idea where the GC is relative to Earth."

Wil leans back in his chair. "Closer than you might think."

"Speaking of," James says, "I'm told that while we were gone, two small frigate class ships buzzed the system."

Wil leans forward. "What?"

James nods. "Yeah, they stayed out near Mars orbit, but we got a good read on 'em. Not ours, for sure, and nothing we've ever seen."

"They say anything?" Wil presses.

James shakes his head. "Nope, ignored all hails. They passed by Mars and kept right on going out of the system."

Wil is about to say something when the intercom chirps. "Wil, Bennie is throwing a fit about the racism in your show," Maxim says.

Wil looks up. "Then his people shouldn't have been slinking around Earth back in the day getting their photos taken."

"They could at least have represented us correctly, then!" Bennie shouts, likely crawling over Maxim. "We're not so spindly! And we don't strut around naked!"

Wil turns back to the comm window on his display. "I better go."

"Don't let Jedi Master Area 51 destroy your ship," James laughs.

Wil smiles. "Will do, and keep me posted on any other visitors. I'll bundle up our ship ID database and send it along in a bit." James nods. The comm window closes.

# CHAPTER 11_

# NOW ARRIVING_

"We've been cleared to land in spaceport Beltral Seven." Cynthia looks back down at her console. "Chevrun Dome." She taps a few controls. Wil's console beeps.

"Got 'em," he confirms, adjusting the *Ghost*'s course. He taps a control and faint lines appear on the primary display. They are green but shift from green to yellow to red, should the ship deviate from the flight plan the space control operator sent them. When Bennie looks over, he says, "Just being safe." The Brailack hacker smiles and turns to look at one of the extra monitors epoxied to the bulkhead next to his station.

On the main display, the fourth planet in the system, cleverly named Kobona Four, fills the screen.

"So, I've been trying to research this Shadow Six," Bennie announces. "Not much on the internex other than some truly inspired conspiracy theories." He holds up a green finger. "But, the dark net is rife with information." He checks one of his displays, then swipes up on it, opening a window on the main display.

"Trying to fly here," Wil grumbles.

"Sorry." Bennie adjusts the size and placement of his new information window. He explains, "According to reports across the GC, these Shadow Six folks are serious players. If what I'm reading is correct," the display updates showing the planet Harrith Prime, "they were called in to clean up the Harrith thing."

"Clean up?" Maxim asks.

"Nothing concrete, but sounds like a lot of those rebels went missing, and the loudest voices in the anti-GC protests afterward also went silent." He looks at Wil. "If this report is to be believed, they were called in when Filhelm had that uprising over import tariffs two cycles ago."

Cynthia makes a whistle-like sound, but her feline featured face doesn't pucker correctly to actually whistle. "That was some nasty stuff."

Maxim nods. "Yeah, I'd heard the rumors that the opposition groups had been aggressively silenced but assumed that was just scuttlebutt."

"Not if even half this stuff is accurate," Bennie says. He closes the window on the primary display. "These guys are serious business."

The *Ghost* enters the upper atmosphere, causing plasma streamers to roll off her deflector shields. The planet below is a mix of whites and grays, with an occasional smudge of black from some factory or another.

Wil doesn't take his eyes off the main display, saying, "Okay, so we land and head into town. I'll meet Nellie at the cafe, you—"

"Nellin," Cynthia corrects.

"Are you sure? Nellie sounds right."

"Certain. Nellin."

"Hmm, okay. I'll meet Nellin at the cafe, and you all spread out. Bennie and Cyn, you try to set up over watch." He takes his eyes off the primary display to look at Maxim. "You two, set up an obvious over watch. You're more well-known and recognizable. Killing sublight engines in five." He puts the repulsor lifts and atmospheric engines into standby as he eases the sub-light engine throttles back.

"Are you trying to out-special-forces, the actual special forces?" Cynthia asks.

"This should end well," Bennie quips.

"Repulsor lifts online. Atmospheric engines online." Wil flips switches, taking the repulsor lifts from standby to active at full power. At the same time, he cuts power to the sub-light engines. The repulsor lifts allow the *Ghost* to coast as the sub-light engines spin down. A press of a button causes the familiar explosion in the aft section as the atmospheric engines ignite. The sudden thrust pushes everyone into their seat backs.

On the main display, the plasma streamers have faded and the clouds have cleared. Several massive domes dot the icy landscape. Each looks to be five or more kilometers in diameter. Some have docking openings, some do not. The green guidance lines on the display are veering starboard toward a dome with a yawning docking bay opening.

The largo rectangle of the docking entrance grows as the *Ghost* drops closer and closer to the dome. "All domes," Wil says to no one in particular.

"Only way to survive here. The surface temp is well below freezing in the warmer seasons and absolutely miserable in the colder ones," Zephyr replies.

"Fun place," Wil quips. The opening in the dome ahead of them now fills the primary display. "Beltral Seven spaceport, dead ahead."

Wil pulls the atmospheric engine throttles back as they approach the dome. By the time the Ankarran Raptor passes through the threshold of the domed spaceport, she's coasting on the antigravity cushion created by the repulsor lifts.

# MAYBE SWITCH TO DECAF_

THE LINE for customs is several hundred beings long. The *Ghost* had sat down on a landing platform halfway up the dome. Landing platforms ring the interior of the cavernous dome. Customs is on the ground level.

Bennie leans to the side. "You're sure we didn't get some type of VIP pass?"

Wil looks down. "You saw the data packet."

Bennie grumbles and moves back into line, glaring at a Malkorite woman behind them.

Wil smiles. "Gabe, comms check. Everyone okay?"

"Affirmative, Captain. Len and the hybrids are accounted for and comfortable. I have placed an order for supplies."

The line moves forward. "All right, sounds good. Hopefully, this won't take too long. Holler if you need anything," Wil says.

"Of course, Captain. Likewise."

"This is taking forever!" Bennie shouts. A Trenbal man in front of them turns and glares at the small Brailack. Bennie returns the glare. "What're you looking at?"

Zephyr pushes Bennie behind her and looks at the reptilian man.

"Apologies. He's constipated." The Trenbal man makes a sour face, looking first at Zephyr then back to Bennie. He harrumphs and turns.

Zephyr turns to Bennie. "I will tape your mouth shut."

Cynthia says, "We're almost to the front."

When Wil steps to the customs official, a blue skinned Brailack, he says, "Hi there."

"Reason for visit."

Wil clears his throat. "Uh, pleasure." He taps an icon on the screen of his wristcomm, sending his travel documents wirelessly to the customs officer.

The small blue being barely looks up from his screen as he looks at the picture of Wil on his screen. "No weapons."

"What?" Wil asks.

The Brailack looks up, sighing. "No. Weapons." He points to a device next to Wil. "Discharge your power cells there."

As Wil pulls both pistols from their holsters, he says, "You make everyone do this?"

"The ones dumb enough to wear their pulse pistols in plain sight, yes." He confirms that the two pistols have had their power cells zeroed out and shouts, "Next."

THE TRANSIT SYSTEM ON KOBONA FOUR IS ONE OF THE MOST efficient Wil has seen outside Tarsis. Just outside the customs area, several platforms with ultra-fast mag-lev trains departing several times an hour wait. The crew board the train heading for the dome their meeting is scheduled to take place in.

"You didn't hide your pistols?" Cynthia stifles her chuckle, sort of.

"Why would I?" Wil protests. "I've never done that before."

Maxim shakes his head. "I guess we need to visit more mid-tier worlds. Pretty standard. You don't brandish, and if you power them down, they don't show up on customs scans." He wiggles a hand. "Usually."

"You tell me this now?"

Cynthia puts a hand on Wil's knee. "We forget you're not from here sometimes." She offers two spare power cells. Wil takes them and leans in to plant a kiss on her cheek.

Wil looks around the transit car. "We're all good on the plan?" He holds up his arm to consult his wristcomm. "The cafe is on a major street, lots of sight lines. There's no reason to expect trouble, but well, it's us." Everyone nods. He flicks something on the screen and everyone else's devices beep. Incoming file.

Bennie looks at his wristcomm. "Looks good to me. From that park, I'll have a good line of sight on you and anyone coming up the street or the feeder street off the park."

Maxim doesn't look at his own wristcomm, having already committed his part of the plan to memory. "It'll take me a few centocks to bypass any locks on the side door of that residential block and get up to the roof." He smiles. "It's low enough that I'll be easy to spot from the street, and likely the spotter will be in the building next to me that is ten floors taller."

Zephyr nods. "I'll be at the table a few tables away from you. Easy to spot."

Cynthia finishes, "I'll be next door enjoying a refreshing beverage." She sees Bennie open his mouth. "I'll get you one before we get started." He grins.

# IT'S JUST COFFEE_

WIL IS SITTING at a cafe table. From what he can see, being under a dome means no business needs indoor seating. The cafe has a small storefront for the kitchen but all the seating is *outside*, even though being under the dome, it is all technically *inside*.

Zephyr is at a table five away from Wil's, closer to the cafe's kitchen entrance. Wil is closer to the street. He spots Maxim moving about the roof of the building across the street. Cynthia is barely visible at the brewery next door. She's sipping a dark grum that looks delicious. She catches Wil looking at her and winks.

"Incoming," Bennie says. Everyone has their earpieces in. Connected to their wristcomms, the small devices are nearly impossible to detect without a scanner.

Wil takes a sip of his chlormax, enjoying the aroma. "This seat taken?" a deep voice rumbles from behind him. The owner moves to stand in front of Wil. An—in Wil's opinion— overly muscled, Tygran man. Where Cynthia is more or less uniformly brown furred, the mass of muscle in front of him is white with black stripes. The man raises an eyebrow as he waits for Wil to answer. Wil coughs and motions to the chair opposite him. "Glad you could make it," the big man says.

Wil nods. "Seemed important, and your bosses said we had to." He grins.

A maybe teenage Olop comes over. "Greetings, do you know what you'd like to drink?" she asks the large Tygran man.

"Chlormax, please," he all but purrs. As the server leaves, he turns to Wil. "Nellin." Offering his forearm.

Wil grasps it. "Wil Calder."

"So, you all think you can break into a Consortium stronghold?"

Wil grins. "Technically, we've already done it once." He shrugs. "Shouldn't be too hard to do it again." The other man cocks his head, studying Wil.

"He's got a friend at the table next to you, Zee," Cynthia reports.

"Max has a friend three floors up," Bennie adds.

Wil nods, then smiles. "Mress says you've got some connections we can leverage?"

Nellin nods once but says nothing as their server returns with a steaming cup of what passes for coffee in the GC. The feline-featured man nods to the young woman.

"Is he as hot as he looks from here?" Cynthia asks.

"So muscly," Zephyr adds.

Wil glares at nothing in particular. Nellin looks over his shoulder. "Your Palorian friends whispering sweet nothings in your ear?"

Wil looks the other man in the eye. "I think we both know we've got friends all over this block."

Nellin nods, smiling. "So, tell me. What's your plan?"

Wil looks around. "Here? Out in the open?" He leans forward. "My understanding is that you've managed to get yourself into the Consortium. Is it a good idea to chat about robbing them in an open-air cafe?"

Nellin takes a sip of his drink. "I expected you to be dumber."

"Thanks?" Wil frowns.

The feline-featured man bares his teeth in a feral grin. "I kind of expected you to bumble into this meeting with no backup."

"Do I need it?"

"Probably not."

"I bet he looks delicious covered in massage oil," Zephyr says over the comms.

"It mats our fur," Cynthia says.

"Then he could rub it on me," the Palorian woman replies. Maxim clears his throat.

"You can rub me in oil," Bennie offers.

Wil rubs his ear, frowning. Nellin grins. "She's right, it does mat our fur." When Wil's eyes snap to his, the other man holds both hands up, "We're definitely better equipped than you. But I'm impressed at your double over watch set up. We haven't even found the one who wants to be oiled up." He makes a dismissive hand gesture. "Anyway, I'm not working for the Consortium. The operatives who are, are nowhere near here. As far as anyone knows, I'm just a guy having a date with another guy."

Wil's frown deepens. "Let's get this over with." He takes a sip, finishing his chlormax. "Here's what we know."

"Good afternoon. I'm Klor'Tillen, and this is GNO News Time." The Brailack journalist is standing with his back to a massive shipworks. Beings and droids of all shapes and sizes are drifting past in zero gravity, working on a ship so huge only a single flat white section is visible.

"I'm here today at the Red Nova Cruise Lines shipyard. Behind me you see," he turns to look over his shoulder, "well, you see a giant bland section of hull plating. The *Galactic Empress* is huge." He holds his small hands as far apart as they'll go. "She'll be the largest non-military vessel in the GC when she launches."

A droid drifts by outside with a large piece of hull in its grippers, the galactic standard version of *ESS* emblazoned across it.

The Brailack journalist continues, "The *Empress* will sport all of the latest entertainments, including two theaters, and nearly thirty different dining establishments with food representing the various worlds of the GC." He smiles, "I know I can't wait to taste what this wondrous vessel has to offer."

# CHAPTER 12_

# ALL ABOUT THAT TRADECRAFT_

After Wil outlines what they've learned about the likely location of the data arcs, leaving out, for now, any mention of a plan, Nellin nods. "Okay, that jives with what we've been able to turn up, more or less."

"More or less?" Wil repeats.

"I'll admit, less. We know that they have several stations like the one you robbed. By the way, that one was an older model. Security set up was well below standard." Nellin winks. "We've been able to discern a few of the names of the stations, but that's it. No locations. No inventories or client lists."

The young server returns. "Would you gentlemen like refills?"

Wil shakes his head. "No, thank you." Nellin shakes his head as well. She puts a small PADD on the table and walks away.

Wil looks at the bill, then Nellin. When the other man doesn't move to pick up the PADD, Wil makes a show of looking at the Tygran man, then the PADD. Nellin sighs and reaches for the device. "One of my people might be perfectly placed to help."

"Do tell."

"She's in scheduling. We can probably get a crate or two sched-uled to be picked up and delivered to Naetu." He puts the PADD down after holding it next to his wristcomm. "That is actually the easy part." He looks at Wil. "More or less."

Wil smiles. "That's a start, for sure."

"Getting you off of the station, that's another matter. Nothing departs those warehouses directly. They've locked things down since your little adventure. No one comes and goes to these stations. Having a membership doesn't include the locations of the storehouses. You set up deposits and withdrawals through the central authority."

"So, what's the problem? You can forge the deposits but not the withdrawals?"

"More or...pretty much, yes," Nellin replies. He continues, "Deposits are pretty generic. Pick up crates somewhere, scan them, deliver to station. Each crate is coded to the client who owns it. The station personnel—droids, we assume—lock it away and transmit a receipt."

"Sounds straightforward," Wil says. "But?" he adds.

"Withdrawals have to come from a Consortium member directly to the managing committee. No ifs, ands, or buts. Face-to-face call submitting the withdrawal request. Approved withdrawals come only from the managing committee."

"Seems...a lot," Wil says.

"It is. The idea being that withdrawals aren't that common. These places aren't banks. You don't put stuff in and take it out on a whim. They're secure, secret storehouses. Withdrawals are big deals, and after yours, the Consortium has had to take security about a hundred times more seriously."

Wil is silent for a moment. "Okay, let's table the getting out part. You sure about the getting in?"

Nellin nods. "Yeah. You'll have to be careful. They're mostly looking for trackers and the like. After that, life signs."

"So, they do scan inbound stuff. Good to know," Bennie says over the comms.

"That's not even how we got in last time," Zephyr adds.

Wil nods along as he listens to his team talk. He smiles, remembering the break-in. He looks at Nellin, who continues, "I think I can get the specifications for the scanners, which should help you work around that."

"Where are things scanned?" Wil asks.

"At the pickup location. Specially designed freighters—again, droid crews, as far as we know—make pickups at designated secure spaceports, secret and remote ports. Once everything is scanned and loaded, the freighters make all due haste to their destination. No detours, no other stops along the way. One pickup per deposit, no mixing."

"Sounds secure."

"It is," Nellin agrees.

"All right. Let me talk to my crew." Wil stands and sees Zephyr and Cynthia stand, along with three others: a Palorian, a Tygran, and a Harrith. The Olop waitress walks over to stand next to Nellin. Wil looks at her. "Nice." She winks.

Bennie trots over to the table, and Nellin snaps his fingers. "Damnit. We knew you had a Brailack but couldn't find him." This time Bennie winks.

Wil continues, "I want to go over this with my crew. How do we reach you?"

"You don't. I'll be here tomorrow afternoon, same table." He gestures to the Olop server. "Toph will be here." The waitress winks at Wil again.

Nellin stands and turns. His people fall in behind him. Several cafe patrons look up from their conversations and caffeinated drinks to watch the group depart.

"Think we can do this?" Bennie asks.

"Do we have a choice?" Wil replies.

# WE CALL IT CRIME_

To ENSURE some privacy while discussing their plans, the crew of the *Ghost* returns to the ship, remaining silent most of the trip to the landing area. Wil watches other passengers as their transit car zips along back to the landing dome.

Cynthia and Zephyr are bringing up the rear as the group approaches the ship. Wil leans toward Maxim. "You know they're talking about hunky cat-man, right?"

"Indeed," the big man growls, looking over his shoulder.

"You guys just need to learn to please your ladies better," Bennie tuts, moving in between them.

Wil and Maxim exchange a look, then punch the small hacker in each shoulder, causing him to yelp. Wil says, "And with that, time to change the subject." He shoves Bennie ahead up the cargo ramp.

The two droids and gaggle of Farsight hybrids are waiting in the hold. They've been busy. The makeshift table they've been using has been replaced with a version that doesn't require taking up the sparring mat. Wil can see that Maxim is happy.

They've also constructed a much more elaborate sleeping area in the other aft corner of the cargo hold.

"You all have been busy," Wil says, looking around.

Len moves forward. "We believed it would make," they turn, gesturing to Jacoby and the others, "them more comfortable."

Wil nods. "Good call. You seem to be feeling more social."

The research droid inclines their head. "I am. Seeing them all alive and well has had a positive impact on me. When I heard Farsight had shut the station down, I had reservations."

Wil rests a hand on the droid's shoulder. "I'm happy you're feeling better." He looks around. "Okay, y'all, time to get down to business." He makes a gesture, beckoning everyone towards the table.

Jacoby walks over. "What's going on?"

Before Wil can answer, a voice from the bottom of the ramp shouts, "Delivery."

Maxim and Cynthia head down the ramp to greet a stout Brailack holding far more food containers than Bennie has ever shown himself capable of carrying. As they head back up the ramp, Wil points to the new dining table. "Planning heists is hungry work."

"A heist?" Jacoby repeats.

Wlen's fleshy head tentacles wave. "Heist?"

T'Kinlo asks, "This the crime you mentioned?"

Breeze sits next to Bol Kar. "What kind of food?"

Bennie takes the seat next to the onetime Palorian woman. "What kind of food do you like?" he purrs.

Wil rolls his eyes. "Our contact recommended this place." He smiles as Maxim and Cynthia set out the food—a veritable feast, now that he sees it laid out. Once the food is spread and everyone is quietly eating, Wil says, "So, I know you all have a notion about what's going on." He looks around to nods from the table. "Len sent us to Meltrom station to save you because they had an inkling of what was ahead of us." He pops a fried morsel in his mouth and chews.

"To be clear, I wanted to rescue you from the station," Len interrupts.

Wil nods. "Well, yeah. That, too, for sure." He watches everyone dig into the assorted dishes arrayed along the communal table, chatting with those nearest them.

After a few minutes, he clears his throat. "Len, would you mind lending me your projector?"

Bennie looks up. "You have a presentation?"

Maxim picks up something breaded and bites into it. "Hope there's no credit stuffed food animal."

Wil sighs. "Piggy bank, and that was one time," Zephyr snorts.

"Captain, I took the liberty of installing a projector," Gabe says from a few feet from the long table. He points up to the ceiling of the cargo hold.

"Oh, hey." Wil follows Gabe's finger. "Neat. Good job." He raises his wristcomm to see the projector on the ship's network. "Bear with me, this is still super rough. I haven't had long."

"So here we are. We know where the data arcs are," Wil says. Nods around the table. "Thanks to our new friend Nellin, we think we have a way onto the station."

"Can you trust him?" Jacoby asks.

"Probably not," Wil admits.

"We don't have a lot of options," Bennie adds. Wil nods.

"How does this involve us?" Wlen asks, her throat sack pulsing nervously, reminding Wil of a frog croaking on a lily pad. If the frog had fleshy head tentacles.

Wil looks at the woman who was born a Brailack but now resembles a Rastafarian frog with ape-like arms. "Well, how big can you get?"

## BRASS TACKS_

Before Wlen can reply, Wil continues, "According to Nellin, they scan inbound cargo on pick up, at specific locations." He points to the hybrids. "You all don't show up on sensors." Most of them nod.

T'Kinlo makes a noise. "So, what? We break into your bad guy space station for you and steal the data archives?"

"We appreciate you rescuing us from that broke down station, but we don't owe you this," Breeze says.

Folit, the used-to-be-Trollack man says, "Owe them?" He points to Wil. "No. Owe it to Farsight to see that no one else suffers like us? Yes."

Maxim and Zephyr both look at Wil, who holds his hands up. "No, yes, I agree...Well, not entirely." He stops, running a hand down his face. "Hear me out."

Bennie tuts. "You have a slide show?"

Wil flips him off.

"Slide show?" Demfley asks, her hover sled bobbing as she eats something off a plate someone placed in front of her.

"Long story," Zephyr says.

Bennie chuckles. "Not that long. He," he points at Wil, still standing at the head of the long communal table, "made a slide show about how we'd break into the first Consortium station. There was an animal stuffed with money—"

"Puggy bank," Maxim offers.

"No, pazookie bank," Zephyr corrects.

"Piggy bank," Wil growls. "Anyway—"

"So, he had this piggy bank, then he had these drawings of us." He gestures to Maxim and Zephyr. "They were horrible. Max had this one eye that was bigger than the other."

"I'm not an artist," Wil protests.

Bennie ignores him. "Then he had a drawing of the station, and there were lines going here and there." His thin arms are cartwheeling all over the place for emphasis.

"Okay!" Wil shouts, drawing everyone's attention back to him. "No slides. Here's the deal. We, all of us, get ourselves aboard the station. We get the data arcs, we get out."

"That's it? Sounds simple," Jacoby quips.

Wil nods. "There's a lot more, and a lot of risk, but like Follicle said—"

"Folit," Folit corrects.

Wil nods. "Sorry. As Folit said, this is to make sure no one suffers."

"And get paid," Bennie murmurs, then makes a pained squeak as Cynthia locks eyes with him.

Wil ignores the Brailack. "Farsight did horrible shit to you; the Consortium will do worse to way more. They operate here on Kobona Four. When they get those data arcs decrypted, this place will be a nightmare. They'll start snatching people off the street until they find just the right formula to make the soldiers that Farsight was trying to make."

Most of the hybrids turn to look at Jacoby, who is sitting perfectly still, his massive arms resting on the table, the smaller set nestled in next to his chitinous exoskeleton. His eyeless face turns from Wil to the rest of the beings sitting at the table. "Some of us could die, probably will die. I know nothing about this Consortium, but if they could steal those data arcs from the GC, they're not to be taken lightly." He turns to Wil, his partially-insectoid mouth moving. "I won't speak for anyone but myself, but I'm in."

"Count on me," Wlen says, her massive mouth forming a wide grin.

"I, too, am in," Demfley says from her hover sled.

Breeze, Sekma, and Folit raise their limbs. The rest of the table follows suit.

# IT'S BIGGER THAN THAT_

TRUE TO HIS WORD, Nellin's associate Toph is waiting at the same table Wil and Nellin had sat at the day before. Wil sits. "Hey."

"Hey back," Toph replies. She raises her arm and says something into her wristcomm. Looking at Wil, she says, "He'll be here in a millitock." She winks and stands.

As she walks away, Wil says, "Hey, can you get me a chlormax?"

"Someone will be by to help you!" She waves over her shoulder, exiting the patio area.

Wil looks at his wristcomm, loading the internex entry for Kobona Four. He's busy reading about the most recently constructed dome, built by a conglomerate of local and off-planet businesses, when a steaming cup of chlormax appears in front of him. He looks up. "Hey, furry."

Dropping into the seat across from Wil, Nellin's eyebrow rises. "So, what's the deal?"

"What's he wearing?" Cynthia purrs. She, Zephyr, and Bennie are sitting in the park nearby. Everyone agreed that over watch wasn't needed, but backup might be.

Wil groans. "We'll need a few days to get things arranged, plus however long it takes to get wherever we need to be for the pickup."

Nellin nods, taking a sip of his drink, "Myself and two others will be joining you." His whiskers twitch from behind the cup.

"The hell you are," Wil counters.

"Non-negotiable. Ask the ladies cutting your checks."

"I don't care what they have to say. I'm saying no."

"Because I'm hunky and your lady friends are into me?"

"He is sexy," Cynthia admits over the channel.

"Very," Zephyr agrees.

"Ye—no. But egotistical dick just moved up the list." Wil waves his hands. "No, we've already got a full cargo hold. We don't have room."

"Cargo hold full of what?" The Tygran man leans forward.

Wil grimaces, realizing his slip. He sighs. He takes a sip of his drink, buying himself time to think of what to say, then blurts, "Mutants made from Source DNA."

"Smooth," Zephyr whispers in his ear.

"This is why we don't tell you things," Bennie says.

"What do you mean, you don't tell me things?" Wil demands.

"What?" Nellin asks. Wil points to his ear. The Tygran man nods and takes a sip of his chlormax. "We'll talk about this later." He turns to Nellin. "Farsight was using alien—"

"Alien?" Nellin repeats.

"Alien-er, DNA from, well, let's just say from far away. They tested various species against their will. The DNA interacted with these people in different ways, none of them good."

"And they're in your cargo hold because...?" the Tygran special operator presses.

"Just bring him to the ship," Maxim says from the *Ghost*.

Wil inhales. "Come on." He doesn't wait for Nellin, standing and walking out of the patio toward the nearest transit station.

"Oh, uh, wow," Nellin stammers as he enters the cargo hold.

"Hi," Bol Kar says, walking by, his multisegmented limbs clicking on the deck of the cargo bay. Sekma is following him and waves, his toothless mouth open in a broad grin.

Nellin doesn't move. His mouth is hanging open. In Wil's ear, Maxim says, "I had them do that." The joy in his voice is obvious.

Wil puts a hand on the muscular Tygran. "Come on, big guy." He guides the man further into the hold.

Jacoby stands up from the communal table. "Hello. I am Jacoby."

"Close your mouth," Wil whispers.

Nellin looks at Wil, then closes his mouth. "Forgive me." He extends his arm. Jacoby clasps the Tygran man's forearm in greeting. The Tygran looks at Wil. "What is this?"

"This is what Farsight was up to," Maxim says, joining them. "Well, at least part of what Farsight was up to."

"And this is what you're hoping to stop? This is what the Councilor is working on?" Nellin asks, following Jacoby to the table.

Wil nods. "It is. The data arcs the Consortium stole contain all of Farsight's research. Their hybridization work, their work on biological armor, like they used on their fleet a while back. The works."

Nellin sits. "Like I said, I'm coming with, now more than ever. This isn't acceptable. We want to help."

"Good morning. I'm Mon-el Furash." The Malkorite journalist is standing in what looks like an observation lounge aboard a starship or space station. "I've just received word from sources that Peacekeeper Command has detected a mysterious fleet in the region of space called the Void. We reported on this earlier and can now confirm. There are ships, they are of unknown origin, and they are believed to be hostile."

She puts a hand to her elephantine ear, causing the jewelry lining it to jingle. "That's true, Megan. From what I'm being told, these vessels don't resemble the ships created by Farsight Corporation. In fact, I've heard, but can't confirm, that these vessels resemble Peacekeeper ships."

She nods, listening to Megan back in the studio. "That's right, it's been a turbulent time lately with mysterious ships and fleets. The Peacekeepers have launched the 8th fleet to investigate. I'm here aboard the Peacekeeper Command station in the Tarsis system, and I'll have more soon."

# CHAPTER 13_

# STOCKING UP_

"I'll get my people started on setting up the deposit," Nellin says as the train back to the habitat dome arrives. He hands Wil a small data card. "That has my direct contact details. I'll be in touch when we're ready, but it shouldn't be more than a day."

Wil slides the data card into one of the inside pockets in his brown duster. "Okay, we'll stock up for extra passengers."

The Tygran special operations team leader steps into the train and moves to blend in with other travelers, quickly vanishing from sight. Wil turns and walks back to the security gate for already cleared visitors to get back to the landing platforms and the *Ghost*.

Wil taps his earpiece. "Gabe, feel like going grocery shopping?"

"I am on my way, Captain," the droid replies.

"So, how's Len?" Wil asks as he steps out of the train that's taken him and Gabe to a dome over a hundred kilometers away from the dome the *Ghost* is parked in.

Gabe follows him off the train, the two of them following the flow of pedestrian traffic out of the station. A sign hanging over the door indicates that the main market district is only a few hundred meters beyond the threshold. "They are doing better. I believe our rescuing the hybrids from the station has had a positive effect on their mental state."

"A good mental state is definitely a plus." Wil points toward an entrance to a massive open-air market.

"Indeed," Gabe agrees.

The market looks like the open-air markets common on many worlds, though being under a dome, it is considerably cleaner than what the crew of the *Ghost* is used to. Each stall is an orderly cube approximately five meters square. Vendors seem to be aligned by offering: several rows of food, technology, housewares, and more.

"Do you have a shopping list?" Gabe asks as they pass vendors hocking home furnishings.

Wil shrugs. "Sorta. It's in here." He taps his temple.

Gabe makes his sigh-like noise. "I see."

Wil reaches up to slap his friend on the shoulder. "Come on, this'll be fun! We haven't hung out, just the two of us, in ages." He heads off to one side of a T intersection, a way-finding sign overhead showing that foodstuffs are to the right. "Oh, look! Crispy yipsee strips!" Wil rushes over to a stall operated by an elderly Olop woman. "They come in other flavors?" He holds up a vacuum sealed bag, shaking it. "Gabe, look. Spicy."

"Hey, hairless, don't crush 'em up!" the small woman growls. Her fur a uniform gray.

"Oh, sorry." Wil blushes. He places the bag back on the shelf. "What other flavors do you have?" Gabe arrives, followed by a grav sled. Wil looks at his friend. "Good call." He turns back to the shopkeeper, leaning forward. "I'll take all the spicy ones." He turns to Gabe, beaming.

The woman grabs an empty box from under the counter next to her, grabbing the sealed packages.

"You should also get the plain. Maxim likes those," Gabe offers.

Wil nods to the woman, who grabs several bags of the plain crispy yipsee strips.

"You have money, right?" The shopkeeper offers the box of snacks to Gabe, who places it on the grav sled. She holds a PADD up for Wil to see the screen.

"I feel like you're overcharging me," Wil grumbles, looking at the screen.

"You can give 'em back," the small, furry woman says, frowning. Wil places his thumb on the reader, accepting the charge. The frown turns to a smile. "Pleasure doing business with you."

As they exit the stall, heading further down the row, Gabe says, "You do plan to purchase actual protein as well?" Wil sighs and turns toward a stall displaying pouches of meat and meat analog products.

# OFF WE GO_

"We're cleared for departure," Cynthia announces. The hybrids are in the cargo hold getting comfortable, while Nellin and his two colleagues are getting situated in the guest berths.

Wil nods. "Off we go." He pushes the power lever for the repulsor lifts forward. The *Ghost* rises more smoothly than normal off her landing struts. Deep inside the ship, the sound of the powerful legs retracting and hull panels closing echoes.

"Very nice." Bennie turns slightly to give Wil a thumbs up. Wil rolls his eyes.

The bridge hatch opens and Nellin walks in. On the main display, the airlock of the spaceport dome is directly ahead. "Nice takeoff. I barely felt it."

Cynthia chuckles, looking down at her console.

"I will crash this ship into the goddamn wall," Wil grates.

Nellin looks around. "Something I said?"

Bennie replies, "He's just sensitive."

Maxim deadpans, "He crashes a lot."

Nellin looks at the back of Wil's head and smiles. He looks around the bridge. "I've never been on Raptor before. Nicer than I would have expected."

"She's seen some upgrades," Wil says without turning around. The spaceport dome is behind them now, the slate-colored clouds filling the primary display.

Nellin nods. "Impressive she's still flying. This is what, an eighty? Eighty-five?"

"She's an eighty-nine," Wil replies, his chest puffed up a bit.

"Nice," the Tygran man says, nodding.

The clouds on the primary display thin, revealing the dark of space beyond. Stars are appearing.

Nellin steps forward toward Zephyr's station. "Here. Our destination." He holds out a small data card. She takes it, inserting it into a reader on her console.

"The Aegoird system?" she says, reading the data.

"The one with the war?" Maxim asks.

"War?" Wil asks. The primary display shows just stars now. The *Ghost* is heading away from the planet to a safe FTL distance.

Nellin nods. "A war ravaged the planet. A civil war. They nuked themselves to oblivion."

"Damn," Wil says. "How come the GC didn't step in?"

"Protected planet," Maxim says. "Like Earth, hands off."

"Like Earth used to be," Cynthia chips in.

Wil shudders. "So if Earth can't get their shit together?"

"The GC will watch them burn themselves to the ground," Bennie says.

"Cheery," Wil says.

"Sending the coordinates," Zephyr says.

"Got 'em," Wil replies. As he inputs the coordinates, he adds, "So we're going to a radioactive wasteland?"

"Yup," Nellin says. "The Consortium has a ground base set up. We'll land, drop off your cargo modules, and take off. The droids at the station will get them ready for pickup."

Wil nods, pushing the FTL control levers forward. The primary display shows the stretchy stars of FTL travel. He turns. "I guess we should figure out how this is gonna work." He looks around. "We're five days out from rageroid—"

"Aegoird," Nellin corrects.

Wil nods. "Yeah, that place. We've got a few things to iron out." He smiles at Nellin. "Do you like tacos?"

# TACOS AND DE-ESCALATION_

"You, Malkorite guy." Wil is pointing and snapping his fingers. Everyone—the crew of the *Ghost*, the hybrids, and Nellin's commando team—are gathered in the cargo hold around the table Gabe has helped create.

The table is just big enough for the new larger complement of the *Ghost*.

"Branx," the man offers.

"Sure," Wil says. "Can you pass the cheese?"

The man looks around the table at the plates and bowls arrayed near him. He shakes his head, his earrings jangling. "I don't know which one that is."

Wil points. Branx reaches for a bowl. "No, not that one. Over, more over, keep going. Okay, yeah, that's it."

Branx exhales, "You mean klorm." He passes the bowl to T'Kinlo, next to him.

Wil nods. "Thanks." He sets about fixing a taco. The table is crowded and noisy with conversations crossing this way and that. He smiles as he watches these various beings interact, some having been together for years, others having just met. Bennie is at the far end hitting on Wlen.

Wil waves at Gabe, who is standing off to the side of the hold with Len. Wil can't tell if they are talking to each other or not. The two droids look like statues. "Presentation time."

Gabe inclines his head. "Of course, Captain. Activating presentation mode."

"Presentation mode?" Cynthia says from her spot next to Wil.

He winks. "I gave Gabe and Len a project."

The harsh industrial lighting of the cargo hold dims, causing the various conversations to come to an end. The illumination drops to about fifty percent of normal, cast upon a section of the back wall of the hold, the only wall with enough space to project an image on, the rest being occupied by pipes, conduits, and wiring bundles.

From the far end of the table, Bennie says, "This is fancy. I hope you upped your game from the version we saw earlier."

Wil raises both fists, middle fingers extended. He gets up from the table and moves to stand near the illuminated square on the wall.

"Where's the projector?" Maxim wonders.

"It must be tucked into the conduits up there," Bol Kar says.

"I think I see it next to that waste return pipe," Toph says, pointing.

Wil's eyes narrow as he takes a deep breath, his arms crossing. "The projector is on the crossbeam, next to the wiring bundle," he grates, pointing it out. He's had this incredibly small projector for years, longer than the crew has been with him. After he bought it, he realized that he had no use for it. The wall display upstairs on the common deck already takes up most of the bulkhead. The projector doesn't add anything. He tried setting it up in his quarters but discovered that there is a resolution at which pornography becomes disquieting.

"Oh, I see it now," T'Kinlo says.

Wil leans against the bulkhead, slowly knocking his head against it.

"Sorry, Wil," Jacoby offers.

Wil opens his eyes. Everyone is watching him now. "Okay, here's what I'm thinking."

Small hand drawn portraits of the hybrids, Nellin and his colleagues, and the crew of the *Ghost* appear.

"I didn't know you could draw," Cynthia says.

Wil nods to the two droids still standing near the large cargo doors. "All Len." He clears his throat. "We can't all go on this job. For one thing, someone needs to fly the *Ghost* out of the area so the Consortium pickup team doesn't see her." An icon appears on the wall, the *Ghost*.

"Plus, you know the ship melting heat and radiation." Maxim offers.

Wil waves the comment away. "Also, I don't think Wlen can hold that many of us." Everyone turns to the Brailack woman, her wide-set mouth in a grotesque grin that scrunches her eyeless face. Her neck sack bulges twice. Toph, across the table from the one-time-Brailack woman, flinches.

"So, here's what I'm thinking." Another icon appears, a space station. "Team A, the team going to the station, is Wlen, obviously. Myself, Gabe, Bennie, Maxim, and Breeze."

"No way," Nellin says. "We're coming with. We're not spending five days cramped up in this scow to then watch you do the job."

"Scow?" Wil demands. "You were pretty impressed earlier."

Nellin waves a hand. "That was before you annoyed me."

PECKING ORDER_

WIL HOLDS his hand up to stop the ensuing argument. "There's only so much room."

"Where?" Nellin demands. He points at Wlen. "You said she was involved. I don't understand."

Wlen sighs. She drags herself away from the table. Before she is a meter away, she's twice the size she was. Within seconds she's four times her original size, showing no sign of stopping.

"What the..." Nellin mumbles.

"So neat," Toph says, getting to her feet.

Massive Wlen looks down. "This is what he's talking about," she says, her voice rumbling through the cargo hold. Her throat sack expands.

"No way." Nellin turns to Wil. "That's what you meant? In... her?"

Wil nods. "Not my first choice, but yeah." He points to the hybrids. "On top of their disfigurement and unique abilities, they don't show up on scanners." He takes a breath. "Wlen gets big, we get in her..." he gulps "...pouch. Then she gets in the cargo module. Gabe says he can mask himself from sensors."

He looks at Wlen, her head bent against the ceiling of the cargo hold. He nods. "Thanks." She nods and begins to return to her normal, more Brailack size. He looks at Nellin. "You didn't let me finish, though. Once we're in, we can signal you."

Toph shakes her head. "From what we know, they'll spot the *Ghost* long before we're close enough to do anything."

"You won't be coming in the *Ghost*," Wil replies. He points to Demfley, her grav sled gently bobbing as she watches the exchange.

"She turns into a starship?" Nellin asks.

Jacoby barks a laugh. "No, but one other thing the Captain didn't mention is that all of us are capable of surviving in vacuum." He points to his friend. "Assuming we can get somewhat close, maybe get a boost from the ship, she can get to the station."

Nellin looks at Branx and Toph. "I guess it's time to get to know our shipmates." Both agents nod.

"Can I finish this?" Wil asks, gesturing to the bulkhead, still showing the portraits, the icon for a space station, and the *Ghost*. "I put in a lot of work on this."

"When?" Cynthia asks, but waves it off when Wil glares at her.

"So, Team A goes in, we secure the station, then call in team B." He looks at Nellin. "Team B is you and your crew, Max, Jacoby, and Cynthia." He looks at everyone else. "The rest of you I'll need here to bail us out with the *Ghost* should things go sideways."

"Is that likely?" Branx asks.

Bennie tuts, then looks at Branx, seeing the man's expression. "Oh, you're serious."

"You know, we never finished talking about our vacation," Cynthia says as she undresses. Dinner and the planning session ended, and while Nellin and his group mingled, Wil and Cynthia made their exit.

After checking the bridge to ensure nothing was amiss and that they were still on course, they came to their quarters.

Wil is sitting at the small desk affixed to the bulkhead. "Yeah, I've been thinking about that. What about Arcadia?"

Cynthia walks over to the clothing fresher, dropping her jumpsuit in. By morning, the device will have cleaned it. "You know, that's not bad. Bennie said it was beautiful."

"And no other people. Well, no other biologicals," he grins, "as Gabe would say."

"I like it." Cynthia ruffles Wil's hair. "You need a haircut."

"I do, indeed." He stands and heads into the refresher, leaving the door open. "I'll talk to Gabe about it later."

Changing the subject as she crawls under the sheets, Cynthia says, "Thoughts on our odds of not dying?"

Wil leans out, toothbrush hanging out of his mouth. "I wunno, I thonk we've got a pruhtty sahlid pwan." Despite the GC having long since gotten to the point of using a simple mouthwash-like solution for teeth cleaning, Wil stocks up on toothbrushes and Colgate when he's on Earth.

Cynthia squints. "Spit and repeat." Wil finishes brushing and repeats what he said. "Ah, I'll grant you, your plan seems pretty solid. Lot of unknowns around the station."

Wil nods. "Yeah, that part kinda worries me, too."

# CHAPTER 14_

# COMING TO TERMS_

"Why are they singing?" Nellin asks. Now that Wil has a projector set up in the hold, he's decided that it's time to introduce the various beings crowded into the cargo hold to some of his favorite things. They have five days, after all. When a riot almost breaks out on their second day over the sitcom *ALF*, he opts for something more pedestrian.

"It's a musical. That's what they do in musicals," Wil repeats for what feels like the fifth or sixth time. He and Cynthia are sitting on a cargo crate off to the side.

"They're singing about revolution?" Breeze asks. She looks at Jacoby sitting next to her. He shrugs as best his insect-like body will allow.

"And being treated poorly. That woman is a sex worker, right?" Bennie says. He's next to Wlen, an arm draped around her.

"Yes, and yes, but she didn't want to be. She had no choice," Wil says, trying to encourage everyone to pay attention to the movie unfolding on the projected display.

"There's nothing wrong with sex work," Zephyr says.

Wil holds up both hands, palms out. "No argument. This is set hundreds of years ago, Earth time. Sex work wasn't looked on favorably then. It was also very dangerous." He points to the screen. "You'll get more from it if you watch it."

Cynthia clucks. Leaning over, she whispers, "I guess we should have let you subject them to *Star Wars*."

"There's still time." He winks. "Just over two more days. We can get through the first twelve, if we eat our meals while we watch." Cynthia groans.

At the end of *Les Misérables*, the expanded crew of the *Ghost* votes to strip Wil of his entertainment privileges. He and Nellin are now sitting at the kitchenette table in the common area, the deck above the cargo hold. Each is holding a bottle of grum. The Tygran man says, "I think we need to iron out a chain of command."

Wil takes a sip of his grum. "Sure, that's easy. I'm in charge." He holds up a hand. "I gave in on you and your team coming along." He shakes his head. "But this is our opp. We were hired to do it. You're an add on. I'm okay working with you. In fact, I think you three will be assets, but this is my ship, my job."

The Tygran man stares, saying nothing. He takes a sip of grum, then nods. "I command my people."

Wil thinks a moment, then nods. "Deal." He extends his arm. Nellin reaches across the table and grasps Wil's forearm. He takes another drink. "You ever wonder what happened after your little stunt in the Harrith system?"

Wil tilts his head. "What do you mean?"

Nellin chuckles. "After you all brought things tumbling down around Janus and his krebnacks' heads, someone had to clean things up." He nods to the refrigeration unit and wiggles his almost empty bottle. As Wil gets up for refills, he continues, "My team and I got sent in to help quiet things down. There were a lot of—thank you." He takes the offered bottle of grum. "There were a lot of upset public officials throughout that sector. Even though the GC was transparent and forthcoming, a lot of the folks out there were screaming for war and reparations and everything in between."

"You're cleaners?" Wil takes a sip of his drink, eyes narrowing as he watches the man across from him.

"After a fashion. We had to calm things down as quickly as we could."

"Chilling," Wil says.

Before Nellin can reply, the hatch to the stairwell opens, and Cynthia walks out. "Ready for bed?"

Wil looks past Nellin to Cynthia. "Yeah, babe, be right there. Everyone done down there?"

She smiles. "Yeah, Folit caught Bennie cheating and spit up some kind of sticky goo all over the little krebnack. Put a damper on the game." She turns back into the stairwell, closing the hatch behind her.

Wil looks at Nellin. "We should clear out before Bennie gets up here. He can be grating when he gets complain-y."

"More grating than normal?" the other man asks. Wil grimaces and nods.

# WELL, THIS IS DEPRESSING_

"Oh, wow," Wil says. On the primary display, the ruined world of Aegoird is slowly spinning. The continent that is visible is pockmarked with craters. "They did that?" He nods to the display.

Maxim nods. "Yeah."

Nellin points to several objects in orbit. "They had begun to explore their system, experimenting with early stage FTL. Stations, and even a few small colonies on their moon, all destroyed. They had yet to unify under a single planetary government, and as some nations progressed faster than others, animosity grew quickly." On the screen, the wreckage of a space station that looks like it would have been three times the size of Earth's ISS 2 drifts past in its orbit, trailing debris and space suited bodies.

Wil shudders, pressing a control on his console. "Gonna record this and send it home. Maybe it'll help keep 'em from destroying Earth."

"Probably not," Bennie says.

Wil looks over his shoulder to Nellin, standing near the hatch. "Where to?"

Nellin steps forward and hands Wil a data card. Wil looks at it. "You just have a stack of these things?" He inserts it into his console.

The anti-virus software Bennie installed alerts him that the card is free of malware. His navigation display updates with a suggested route. "Just droids? They won't sound an alarm?"

Nellin shakes his head. "Yup and nope. There's a staging area with approved empty modules. We land, drag the ones we want aboard. Fill them up and leave them. The droids will come out once we leave and do their thing."

"Uh, I've got a ship on scanners," Zephyr announces, looking up from her console. She taps a command and a window on the primary display appears, showing a trio of blocky freighters. The thing looks abandoned, sitting at the Lagrange point between Aegoird and its only moon. "Now three, no life signs."

Nellin looks at the display. "My operative in scheduling mentioned something about the Consortium keeping automated freighters nearby. If she's right, the moment we leave the depot's sensor range, they'll summon one of those things to pick up our cargo."

"Quite the operation," Cynthia says. Nellin nods.

Wil taps a control on his console, dismissing the window showing the freighter. "Here we go." He accepts the new course and watches as the small green lines appear on the main display, guiding the *Ghost* toward the coast of the pockmarked continent.

"The base is on a hilltop near that mountain range. The radiation is not as bad at the higher elevations," Nellin says.

"Oh, good," Cynthia says. She adds, "We got the challenge from the automated satellite. Looks like the codes Nellin's team in the Consortium gave us, worked." She glances up at the hulking Tygran special operator.

"I'll go let the others know to get ready," he says, opening the bridge hatch.

When the door closes, Wil looks around. "We ready to do this?"

"You mean ride to a secret space station inside the neck pouch of a mass shifting mutant?" Bennie asks.

THE *GHOST* FLIES OVER THE REMAINS OF A CITY DEVASTATED BY war. One of the craters they had seen from orbit bisects the remains. The part of the city left standing is a mix of ruined and blasted buildings. Several towers that might once have reached the clouds now lay tumbled across streets amid smaller buildings. Few buildings are still standing.

"God, this could be New York," Wil says as they roar over the crater toward the low-lying hills at the base of the coastal mountain range ahead of them. The navigation path is still guiding them toward the landing area of the automated cargo depot.

Wil looks over to Zephyr. "Anything?"

She looks over. "Not a thing. If we didn't get the navigation details from that satellite, there'd be no telling anyone was here."

"Because no one is supposed to be here," Maxim adds.

"Wouldn't people come to loot this place? I mean, surely something survived the apocalypse."

Maxim replies, "Oh, I'm sure some have braved the radiation." He shrugged. "The Aegoirdians certainly won't complain."

"Being dead and all," Bennie adds.

Wil looks at him. "Did you think I didn't get what he was saying?"

The Brailack shrugs. "Sometimes you can be dense." He ducks as a small bean bag smacks against one of his monitors. Wil keeps a small supply of them at his console after breaking a second Kel statuette by throwing it at Bennie.

IT'S WARMER THAN I EXPECTED_

The landing pad is exactly as Nellin said it would be. "I told you so," he says as the cargo ramp clangs to the pockmarked metal deck of the Consortium cargo depot. He and Maxim are clad in environment suits.

Maxim points to a section of the landing pad full of cargo modules of various sizes. "How come the criminals don't bring their loot in their own cargo modules?"

Nellin walks down the ramp. "It's all about trust." He turns to look up at Maxim. "No one in the Consortium trusts anyone else. After Xarrix's stunt, these depot stations aren't messing around." He points to the modules they are approaching. "These are securable by each member but designed to be fully scannable by the droids here and the droids receiving the modules on the station."

They reach the assorted modules, and Maxim rests a hand on the biggest one, nearly five meters to a side. "How do we get this," he raps a knuckle on the large cargo crate, "into the ship?"

Nellin points to the bottom of the module, then walks around the corner, out of sight. A second later, the entire module rises from the landing pad. Nellin leans back around the corner, "Built in grav sleds. Able to be remotely disabled." He nudges the module toward the *Ghost*.

"Neat," Maxim says, moving to take up a position to help guide the massive cargo module toward the *Ghost*'s ramp.

Watching the two men guide the module toward the ship, Wil turns to Wlen. "You ready?"

She sets her wide mouth in a grim line, throat sack fluttering. Her eyeless face turns to Wil. "No, but do I have a choice?"

The module glides through the static atmosphere barrier that keeps the cargo hold atmosphere in while the massive doors are open. As Maxim and Nellin cross the threshold of the barrier, the side of the module within the cargo hold splits down the middle and slides apart.

Wlen moves to the module, looking inside the cavernous space. "This will not be fun." She turns her eyeless face to the others, fleshy tentacles twitching. "For any of us." She's already three times her normal size. She backs the rest of the way into the module. She is now filling the entire thing, leaving only a meter between her face and where the two panels will come together to form the side of the cargo module. "All aboard," she croaks, her voice deeper than Maxim's. She opens her mouth, her throat pouch expanding.

Wil closes his visor, sealing his armor. "Ready, Jarvis?" He picks up a small cargo module that they've packed with specially designed food that Zephyr assures them is almost completely digestible, resulting in less need to relieve themselves in their armor. Nellin swears the trip should only be a few days, but Wil counters with *just in case*. The module also contains replacement water canisters for the various armor systems being worn.

"I am, sir. This should be an exciting adventure," the armor's AI replies.

Wil makes a face. "Something like that." He turns to Bennie, who is closing up his own armor. "Ready, pipsqueak?" Bennie nods.

Gabe comes over, holding Maxim's Peacekeeper Scout armor. "You can change en route."

Maxim looks around. "Yay?"

Wil shrugs and turns to Jacoby. "Can you get this thing back out on your own?"

Jacoby says, "I can help."

Nellin quirks an eyebrow. "I didn't see environment suits in your size...or shape."

Cynthia smiles. "They don't need air."

"What?"

Jacoby holds up three clawed hands. "I mean, we do, but we can go without for a bit." He makes an expression that might be a smile, his mandible-type jaws shifting.

Wil shudders. "Let's go." He shoves Bennie and Gabe toward the gaping mouth of Wlen.

Breeze comes up alongside him, a hacked together comm set on her head. She grins.

The crate shudders. They can feel it through the skin of Wlen's throat pouch. Maxim looks at Wil. "I'm having second thoughts." The crate shudders again, likely moving from the *Ghost*'s cargo ramp to the landing pad.

Over the team comms, Cynthia says, "See ya when we see ya."

# NEWSCAST_

"This just in," Megan says, taking her seat hurriedly behind the news desk. She picks up a PADD, glancing at it. "We've just heard from our colleague, Mon-el Furash: the alien fleet discovered in the Void has engaged the Peacekeeper 8th fleet. They are indeed hostile and appear to have ill-intent towards the GC."

She straightens herself out and shuffles things on the desk before then continues, "Mon-el is working on getting aboard one of the carriers heading to the front but passed this on to our regional affiliate on Tarsis." Megan is replaced by a video showing Peacekeeper vessels battling what appear to be modified Peacekeeper vessels. The aggressor vessels are mottled black with bulbous chitin-like protrusions, mostly over sensitive areas like engine exhausts and the bridge. The weapons clusters are similarly protected. Peacekeeper weapons glance off the unusual armor as their weapons burn into their opponents. The video ends as a Peacekeeper cruiser explodes.

Megan shudders. "Stay tuned."

# PART FOUR

# CHAPTER 15_

# TIME TO GET TO WORK_

The *Ghost* lifts off the criminal cargo depot landing pad and accelerates up and out of the atmosphere as quickly as possible, atmospheric engines roaring.

A heavy door in the depot building slides open with a loud groan. Two droids walk out. Both are identical: bipedal with thin torsos and oversized heads. Lenses and optical sensors cover the front of their heads. The left arm of each droid ends in what must be a sensor apparatus, probes of various types stick out of them.

The droids circle the cargo module twice each, their scanner arms pointed at the module. After their careful examination, they return to the depot.

An hour passes before one of the nondescript freighters that the crew of the *Ghost* had seen earlier descends on powerful repulsor lifts. The freighter has no visible cockpit or windows. A large rectangular hatch slides open as the ship lowers over the module. A thick mechanical arm reaches out to pull the module up into the freighter.

As the hatch closes, the blocky ship rises back into the sky. It never even touches the cargo deck of the depot.

As the module shifts and knocks around, Wil looks at the others. "Guess we're on our way."

Bennie sits down. "Who brought the games?"

Wil produces a deck of cards.

Maxim slips off his environment suit. "Oh my. That's not a pleasant smell."

From everywhere and nowhere, a grumbling "Sorry" booms.

The big Palorian man gets into his armor as quickly as he can. "No offense meant, Wlen." His dented armor slips on easily, panels sliding into place and locking as he adds pieces.

Wil deals out cards to everyone on the food crate in the middle of their little circle. "Wlen, you're out, right?" The enormous throat pouch they're sitting in shifts. "Sorry."

"Now what?" Nellin asks from the bridge hatch.

Zephyr looks over her shoulder, from Wil's command chair. "We go back in, access the sensor beacon we left in orbit, and hope Bennie and Gabe did their jobs." She manipulates the controls, turning the ship back toward the distant star of the Aegoird system.

Cynthia watches the screen as the *Ghost* makes its short FTL jump back down the gravity well. She looks at Nellin. "You think it's about a week?"

He nods, walking to Zephyr's station. He looks to her before sitting down. "These seats aren't very comfy."

Zephyr pulls back the FTL control. The stretched-out stairs of FTL return to normal, the planet Aegoird directly ahead of them.

Cynthia taps a button on her console. "Sending the recognition code."

An indicator on Zephyr's, currently Nellin's, console lights up. "Uh, one millitock." He looks around the console, then turns to Zephyr. "Sensor buffer?"

Zephyr sighs. "Top left, next to the tactical sub-system monitor."

Nellin nods. "Ah, got it." He nods and works the controls. "Here we go. Data stream coming in."

Zephyr looks over her shoulder at Cynthia, who shrugs.

"Sending the flight path to your console," Nellin announces. Maxim's empty tactical console beeps. "Oops. Sending to your console," Nellin says again.

This time the flight control console updates with the incoming data. Zephyr grins. "Got it." She makes a few adjustments. "Here we go." She pushes the FTL control all the way forward.

The bridge hatch opens, and Len enters. "Hello."

Cynthia looks up. "Hi, Len. You doing okay?"

The droid inclines their head, optical sensor lenses spinning. "I am well. I sensed that we had gone to FTL. Did the beacon Gabe and Ben-Ari created succeed in its task?"

Cynthia smiles, nodding. "Yeah. We got a bead on the freighter and we're following."

The droid dips their head. "That is good news. I have prepared a meal for the remaining hybrids. Would you like me to bring something to you, or...?"

Zephyr smiles as she makes some adjustments to the console. "No, we'll join everyone. This is going to be a slow pursuit, to say the least."

"I have to pee," Bennie whines for what, to Wil, feels like the one-thousandth time.

"Then pee," Wil replies, not looking up from his wristcomm, which has an episode of *Married with Children* playing on its small screen. He doesn't love the reboot, but is giving it a shot.

"I'm full," the Brailack replies. Breeze, standing next to the little hacker, takes a step away.

"I told you to watch your water intake," Maxim scolds.

Bennie apes his large friend's reply, then says, "Whatever, I gotta go."

From all around them, the booming voice of Wlen says, "Do not urinate inside me."

The cargo module shudders once, causing everyone standing to shift their feet a bit. It shudders again. Wil looks at Bennie and shrugs.

"Perhaps we have arrived," Gabe offers. "I am detecting a difference in gravity."

Maxim stands up, resting his hand against the fleshy wall of the space they've spent four days in. "Something is definitely happening out there."

Wil looks up. "Wlen, can you hear anything?"

"You know, you're literally inside her? Why not look down when you talk?" Bennie says, shifting from one foot to the next.

Wil turns, both hands in front of him, middle fingers extended. "Start a timer."

"What am I? A clock?" the Brailack hacker replies.

Wil rushes forward and punches him lightly in his midsection. "I was talking to Jarvis."

"That made me pee a little, you drennog!" He does a little dance, shaking one leg.

Breeze sighs, looking at Maxim. "Do they ever stop?"

The big man shrugs. "Not that I've seen."

"So exhausting."

"You've no idea."

Gabe turns in a slow circle. "I am as certain as I can be that we are now inside the station. Or at least no longer in the freighter."

"Can you detect anything outside the module?" Breeze asks, flexing her long thin fingers nervously.

Gabe shakes his head. "Unfortunately, these modules are exceptionally well designed. I am limited to sensing the vibrations coming from the walls. All of my sensors are being blocked. I believe they offloaded us from the freighter, then moved through the station briefly. Wherever we are now, nothing seems to be affecting the cargo module." He looks up, mimicking Wil. "Wlen, are you able to hear anything? Your hearing is likely quite well developed."

From all around them, "I heard footsteps a few microtocks ago, nothing since. Before that, a lot of scraping."

Gabe nods. "I do not think we will get any better confirmation than that."

Wil nods. "Okay, Wlen."

The fleshy room they're in trembles. "Sorry, hold on." The throat pouch contracts. Above them, Wlen's wide mouth opens. Everything around them is contracting.

As the space inside her neck pouch shrinks, her occupants climb and fall out of her open mouth into the cargo module. None manage to exit gracefully.

The moment the mutated Brailack woman is back to her normal size, Bennie demands that everyone face front. Wil looks over his shoulder. "If any of that trickles this way..." He leaves the rest of the threat open ended.

"Whatever, face forward!" Bennie shouts.

While Bennie is busy, Gabe kneels at the hatch to the module and transforms his right hand into a plasma torch. He points the device at the hatch before him. A nearly invisible beam leaps out, burning through the metal. Small puffs of smoke waft. As his hand returns to its normal configuration, he raises his left hand, a single data tendril extending from the tip of his index finger. The thin filament snakes through the still glowing hole.

Gabe looks up over his shoulder. "We are indeed in the storage facility." The data tendril withdraws as he stands. "Five modules up."

"Oh, goodie," Wil quips. "Climbing."

BREAKING AND ENTERING_



"Clear left," Maxim says.

"Clear right."

Wil looks around. They are in a massive room. Three of four walls are lined with modules similar to theirs, stacked nearly twenty high with room to spare. Every few modules, there is a space, showing the support structure for all the modules. He whistles. "This place must be huge." He turns to look at the rest of the team emerging from the crate. "This room alone seems bigger than the Barsoom station."

Bennie nods, joining him. "Guessing since clients aren't allowed to visit their goodies, they consolidated space. I bet there are at least two more of these rooms, maybe three, centered on a central receiving hub."

"Bennie is mostly correct," Gabe adds. "Now that we are free of the sensor jamming of the cargo module, I can confirm that we are in one of four arms of this station. There is a central column through that hatch and down a short corridor. The docking area is below us." He turns to Wil. "I am detecting at least thirty droids present. It is likely that there are more, beyond the range of my sensors."

"What kind?" Breeze asks.

"I cannot be certain," Gabe answers.

"Do they know we're here?" Wlen asks. She is back to her normal, more Brailack size, tentacles waving slightly.

"Not that I can determine." Gabe looks around the room. "The encryption on the wireless network is beyond military grade. I am working on cracking it." He points to a pedestal just inside and to the left of the large hatch that leads to the station proper. "I may be able to access core systems through that pedestal." He moves towards the device.

Bennie follows Gabe. "Need a hand?"

The droid nods. "Of course. Your expertise in breaking into secure systems would be invaluable. My subroutines, while state-of-the-art, are not you."

Bennie beams. "Ah, thank you." He raises his arm and starts typing on his wristcomm. Wil overhears and rolls his eyes.

Maxim and Breeze move off in opposite directions to explore the storage room, each avoiding the pod that Bennie visited earlier. The space is cylinder shaped: twenty plus modules high and ten in circumference. Each module is closed and locked except for theirs. Above, in the center of the ceiling, a massive arm that moves modules in and out of their racks rests.

"Jarvis, can you work on trying to figure out how to contact our friends while Gabe tries to find the data arcs?"

"Of course, sir," the chipper AI replies.

"Captain, I am afraid this pedestal is not on the station network. It appears that each storage arm is a local network unto itself. This pedestal only contains an encrypted copy of the client identifier attached to each module, nothing more."

"Guess we should have known it wouldn't be that easy," Wil says, looking at the hatch. It's big enough to allow a module like the one they came in to pass through with almost a meter on each side to spare. "There's probably a central control area where a master list is kept. Since we don't know the identifier the Consortium uses for their own goodies, we'll have to find that first, then search the arms."

"While avoiding a couple dozen droids whose job is to defend this station," Bennie adds. Wlen says nothing but nods and points to the other Brailack in agreement.

Maxim walks back to stand closer to everyone. "And not causing anything to alert the Consortium to our presence or that there's anything wrong with this station."

"Is that all?" Breeze says. She looks around the space they are in. "I know you all are experts at this, but I'm not seeing a lot of options."

"Experts?" Bennie chuckles.

Wil punches him in the shoulder. "Experts might be an overstatement, but we'll figure it out." He grins. "It's what we do."

"We're doomed," Wlen moans as she moves to stand next to her friend.

Wil makes a face, then walks over to join Gabe at the pedestal. "Can this thing at least give us a station layout?"

Gabe inclines his head. His hand is resting on the pedestal just below the touch screen. Data tendrils are snaking out of his fingertips, penetrating the edges of the screen, causing it to flicker, leaving glitchy artifacts on the display. The tendrils wriggle and pulse as they penetrate the pedestal's systems. The screen blinks and displays a schematic of the station. "We are here." A red dot appears in one of the storage arms.

The station is as massive as Wil assumed. Each arm is the size of the one they are in with a fifty-meter connecting walkway. At the top of the station, a diagonal arm rises from each storage module to what must be the central control center. At the bottom, connected only to the central column, is the docking section. Unlike the station they broke Gabe out of, this one has ships dock inside a large hangar that has a heavy lift off to the side to bring the modules up to the receiving area. Plenty of room for the *Ghost*. Wil does not see any airlocks.

The upper section looks like it is primarily accessed via the central column lift. Wil taps the diagonal arm that leads from the top of their storage area up to the control section. "What's this?"

The image pans and zooms in on the upper section of the storage arm. The droid turns to Wil. "I believe it is our way in." He smiles his uncanny valley smile, making Wil shudder.

# TIME TO HIDE_

Breeze beats her wings as she examines the mechanical arm mounted to the ceiling. She circles the base of the arm several times, then returns to the deck. "There is a control panel up there and a vent covering."

"Then that's our way out of here," Wil says. He looks up, then to Gabe. "Can you override the arm?"

Gabe walks to the pedestal, accessing it with data tendrils again. "Yes."

The large mechanical arm powers up. The two-pronged manipulator lowers to the ground with a clang.

Everyone jumps, several turning their faces to the large hatch expectantly.

"That was subtle," Maxim says.

"Apologies," Gabe says, withdrawing his hand from the pedestal. "The controls are not very well tuned."

Wil quirks an eyebrow. "Can you tell if the droids are moving?"

Gabe pauses, head tilted. "They are. We should move." He moves away from the pedestal. "I can carry Wlen and Bennie."

Breeze flexes her hands, the thin membrane between her long

fingers rippling before going taut. "I can probably carry the Captain." She looks at Maxim. "Sorry."

Maxim looks around. He turns to Gabe. "Toss me."

"I am sorry." Gabe has Bennie in one hand and a shrunk down Wlen in the other. She is now no bigger than a softball.

Maxim points to the cargo module they arrived in. "Toss me."

Wil looks at Maxim, then Gabe. "I don't know..."

Gabe sets the two Brailack down, handing Wlen to Bennie. He walks over to Maxim and grasps the big Palorian man's armored belt and shoulder pauldron. Without a word of warning, he hefts Maxim, crouches, and hurls the big man at the open cargo module they came in.

Wil's eyes go wide.

"That was an impressive throw," Jarvis says in Wil's ear.

Wil nods. "Let's go."

Above them, the doors of the cargo module are swinging closed. Gabe grabs the two Brailack and ignites the thrusters in his feet and calves. Breeze flaps twice to get airborne and wraps her legs around Wil's waist. As she lifts him off the ground, he screams. She shushes him.

Gabe deposits the two Brailack near the mechanical arm's main control junction. Data tendrils snake out of his fingertips, retracting the arm to its default stored position near the ceiling, while Bennie works on the vent covering. Breeze drops Wil next to Wlen on the arm control junction. There is not much room on the narrow support structure.

Gabe moves next to Bennie. "We must hurry. We have thirty microtocks at best."

"I'm hurrying!" the hacker hisses, working a stuck clasp. The grate swings down. "Let's go!" he hisses.

Gabe reaches down for Wlen as Bennie scurries up the shaft. As she climbs up behind Bennie, Wil follows with Breeze on his tail. Gabe moves into the shaft, closing the grate behind him just as the large hatch below opens.

Three droids, similar to the models that scanned the module on Aegoird, flanked by four military grade combat droids, enter the storage module, fanning out. Gabe activates a low-grade energy field to act as a dampening field should the scanner droids turn their attention on the ceiling.

The security droids move around the perimeter of the module before taking up positions in front of the open hatch. The scanner droids make a slow circuit of the space, sensor arms moving up and down.

Gabe looks up at the others, clinging to the sides of the duct, placing a finger to his lipless mouth. Nods from everyone.

Gabe turns to watch the action unfolding below. One of the security droids is examining the pedestal with a scanner droid. The rest are examining various cargo modules. The arm begins to move, lowering to the deck, then moving through what seems like a series of diagnostic movements.

One of the scanner droids moves to the center of the room, aiming its sensor-loaded arm straight up. Gabe can detect the energy of the sensor beams, doing his best to dampen and deflect that energy. Heat builds in the cramped duct.

Several long and uncomfortable minutes pass before the droids depart the storage area. As the large hatch below bangs closed, Gabe looks up at his friends. "I apologize for the heat. Generating the dampening field was quite taxing on my power systems. I will need some time before I am at full capacity again."

Wil looks down. "Let's get Maxim and get moving. You can recover on the move. It looks like this conduit runs about fifty meters."

Gabe nods. "That is correct." He eases the vent covering aside, letting it swing free on its hinge. He holds his hand out, accepting a spool of high-test cable from Wil. Igniting his thrusters, Gabe drops from the duct, arcing toward the cargo module they had arrived in.

# CHAPTER 16_

# WAITING AND WATCHING_

The *Ghost* spends four days keeping the automated freighter just inside its long-range sensor envelope, running its stealth systems at full power to make sure the freighter never knows it is being followed. It has been taxing on the ship's power plant. By the time they arrive in the red giant star system, several of the *Ghost*'s systems are in the red.

"How did Wil do this without a crew? Without Gabe?" Zephyr wonders aloud as they drop from FTL. She and her mismatched crew have spent the entire trip making adjustments and keeping things from overloading. Ahead of them, the freighter is moving into dock with a station that would dwarf the one she and Maxim helped Wil break into cycles ago. At some point in the past, the Consortium apparently stopped using the shield ships Duch had mentioned. Upon entering the system the freighter deploys a large curved shield in front it. The edges of the massive dish trail thick cables, likely designed to dissipate heat.

Nellin shrugs. "I have no idea, but we better move off so we can kill the stealth systems before they break down completely."

Zephyr adjusts their course toward the burnt husk of what likely was a habitable planet billions of solar cycles ago, before this star went into its giant phase.

Zephyr looks at the ceiling. *Now he's got me doing it.* "T'Kinlo, are you able to make repairs to the stealth systems?"

The one-time-Trenbal engineer grumbles over the intercom, "I'll see what I can do. No promises."

"That's T'Kinlo for yes," Jacoby offers from the bridge hatch. His other senses have more than made up for his lack of eyes, but working bridge consoles is not something the original Source DNA seems to have factored for. It leaves him to be a bystander near the hatch.

"How does he work in this mess? Something is stuck to my butt," Toph complains from Bennie's station. The Olop woman plucks something from the seat of her trousers, depositing it on the floor next to her.

Zephyr shrugs. "You wanted to be helpful..." She's sitting in the command station in the center of the bridge. *I could get used to this.* She smiles to herself.

The Olop woman growls, pushing something off a console onto the floor. Nellin chuckles from Zephyr's normal station. He says, "I've got something on long range."

Branx is sitting at Maxim's tactical station. He consults his display. "I think it's a patrol."

Cynthia looks at Nellin. "You didn't say anything about patrols."

He turns. "I don't run the Consortium. My operative is in scheduling. You're lucky I got you what I did."

Zephyr sighs. "We can't stealth, so we're going to have to evade them the old-fashioned way."

"Which is?" Branx asks.

Zephyr taps a few controls as the *Ghost* enters a polar orbit above the cinder of a planet. "Going dark." She looks at Nellin, then over her shoulder to Cynthia. "I don't like it, but you all should get going. Once we start playing villip and rogar with that patrol, getting you launched will be more difficult." The Tygran man nods, looking around. "Okay, let's go."

Toph and Branx stand, as does Cynthia. The latter looks at her friend. "You sure you're good?"

Zephyr shrugs. "We're in it now. We'll be fine. I'm more worried about you all floating without a heat shield."

Nellin looks at his people. "Branx, stay here. She'll need someone with some history on tactical." The Malkorite man nods, sitting back down.

Cynthia nods and pushes open the bridge hatch. Jacoby is the last to depart. He turns. "I'll send you some help." He doesn't wait for her answer, closing the hatch behind him.

The bridge lighting shifts to a dim red.

A few minutes later, Cynthia says over the intercom, "Good luck." She and the boarding team are in the cargo hold.

The bridge hatch opens and the three hybrids slink and creep their way onto the bridge. Zephyr looks over her shoulder, then smiles and looks at the ceiling. "You, too." She turns to the new arrivals. "Okay, I need one of you on sensors and one on comms." She looks around. "If anyone has particular computer skills..." She points to Bennie's station. "There."

Bol Kar moves to Bennie's station, easing his arachnid-like body into the seat. Sekma drops into the seat at the sensor station. Several of the spines that protrude from his body puncture the seat, eliciting a wince from Zephyr. Folit drops into Cynthia's seat, tentacles moving across the controls.

Zephyr watches them get comfortable. "Okay, then."

OUTSIDE THE *GHOST*, A GROUP OF ARMORED AND UN-ARMORED beings are clutching the shell of a space sea turtle that is puffing small jets of air from the tips of its flippers. The odd assault force makes its slow way toward the space station wrapped in an insulating blanket that Gabe fabricated. According to the droid the heavy covering would not only help block the star's heat, but would further shield the assault team from sensors.

The hybrids' being naturally invisible to most sensors makes for great shielding. While they approach, Nellin, Cynthia, and Toph cling to Demfley's underside, keeping her body between the station and themselves. Jacoby is riding on her back. All of them ensconced in the protective blanket. When forming the plan to rob the station, Wil had joked about "Bug Man and his trusty steed." No one laughed.

Since Nellin hadn't been able to get any details on the station's sensor capabilities, suit thrusters were out, and keeping the non-hybrids out of sensor range was a *just in case* decision. To be safe, Cynthia, Nellin, and Toph are keeping their suits powered down to minimum levels, as well.

Back on the bridge, Zephyr turns to Sekma. "Make sure every-thing is set to passive."

The spiny Sylban seems to look at his console, then turns his eyeless face to Zephyr and shrugs.

She bites her lip, looking at her four-bridge crew. "Okay, change. You," pointing at Sekma, "comms." She turns to Folit. "You, sensors." She turns to Bol Kar. "You, you can see your console, right?" He nods, making a chittering sound.

Folit gets settled at the sensor station, quickly scanning the console. "All good. I think."

Zephyr gets up. "You think?"

He shrugs, tentacles wiggling. He moves to let her look at the console. She nods, tapping a button to send the passive sensor data to a large window in the primary display. She turns and smiles.

The patrol craft appears to another droid ship, automated like the freighter which is now departing the system along the course it came in on, having made its delivery.

Dropping into the command chair, Zephyr says, "How many patrols do you think they have?"

Bol Kar turns. "I hope just the one."

## PENTHOUSE_

It takes nearly an hour to climb from the storage area up the diagonal shaft to what the team is pretty sure is the control center. The crew of the *Ghost* all have armor that can adhere to the ducting, but Breeze and Wlen have to get help as their mutated limbs can't find any purchase on the almost perfectly smooth interior of the duct.

It is easier for Wlen, who sheds mass until she can ride on Maxim's back. Breeze sort of rides and straddles Wil as he slowly moves along the conduit, bracing himself with his hands reaching across the width of the duct.

As far as Gabe can tell, the station's droids have returned to their duties. He can't detect any change in the station, though without wireless network access, he is limited to his sensors, which are forced to remain mostly passive while his power systems recover from creating the dampening field he used earlier to hide their presence from the scanner droids.

"Are we—" Breeze starts to ask.

"I will push you off and let you slide all the way to bottom if you finish that question," Wil growls. Under his breath, he says, "Jarvis?" Breeze shuffles, adjusting her position on his back, a long arm wrapping over his shoulder down and around his torso.

The suit's AI whispers, "We're about five meters from the end of the conduit, sir."

Wil nods. Up ahead, the conduit turns a forty-five-degree angle to level off. A meter from the bend, there's a spinning fan. Wil looks around. "Why the fuck is there a fan blade? What the hell?" He helps Breeze off his back so she can perch on the ledge created by the bend in the conduit.

From further back in their group, Bennie says, "Like in that crappy vid you like, Universe Quest? No, Galaxy Quest, right?" Wil makes a face. The Brailack adds, "At least it's not the chompers."

Gabe shifts as he nears the end of the conduit. "I had wondered why there was atmosphere aboard this station." He turns to the others. "I am detecting a single life form." He tilts his head and looks at Wil. "Booyakasha."

Wil makes a face. "Booyakasha?"

The droid nods, pointing toward where Bennie is further down the conduit, waiting. "Our intrusion efforts have finally cracked the encryption on their wireless network."

Wil smiles. "Booyakasha, indeed. What can you tell us?"

"What's going on up there?" Maxim demands. Wil waves him off.

The fan blade comes to a stop. Gabe says, "These conduits exit into an outer ring around the command center. Used to house life support and other equipment." He reaches past the now motionless blade to push open the vent grate. "I have disabled the sensors in the equipment ring. We should still proceed with haste, just in case." He slips past the fan. Breeze, then Wil, follows. Bennie and Maxim climb out, the latter placing Wlen on the deck. Gabe reaches behind the big Palorian to close the grate, the fan blades coming to back to life.

"What now?" Breeze asks.

Wlen has moved a few meters down the curving corridor. "Can we get into the control center from here?"

Gabe tilts his head. "Yes, there is a hatch halfway around the perimeter. The living caretaker is there. The control center is a dwelling." He turns to look at the others. "According to the records, a new caretaker arrives every solar cycle to replace the previous."

"The Consortium must not fully trust their droid work force," Bennie says. "Keeping a single biological in the mix is likely a fail-safe." He smiles. "Smart."

"Your appreciation for their evil deviousness is noted," Wil quips.

Bennie shrugs. "Game recognizes game." Breeze sighs.

Maxim moves to smack the hacker in the back of the head, but Bennie ducks and scurries out of reach.

"Children..." Breeze scolds.

Wil nods. "We have to get to the comms, call in the cavalry." He turns to Gabe. "Lead the way."

## BRING THE NOISE_

"Okay, this is an improvement," Bennie says, stretching, his armored limbs creaking. Breeze follows suit, extending her arms and stretching the thin membrane between her fingers. She flaps twice. Bennie turns to her and gapes.

"Okay, let's get going. Team B is waiting and I don't know how long they or we can go undetected," Wil says, walking down the curved corridor toward the hatch that Gabe says will give them access to the interior of the control center of the station.

The hatch is nondescript and locked. Wil looks at Gabe, then Bennie. "Thoughts?"

Bennie speaks first. "We can lock down internal comms, but the outbound comm system appears to be isolated on a separate system. Which means there's probably a panic button."

"So, move fast," Maxim says.

"I can go in and scout around," Wlen offers as she shrinks before their eyes.

"Still creepy," Wil says, turning away. He looks to Gabe. "Can you tell how many and where?"

Gabe moves to the hatch and stands there a moment before turning. "Unfortunately, no. There is a damping field running through this bulkhead. I can detect the biological, and what must be droid power cells, but that is it. I cannot get more detailed."

"Okay, here's the plan," Wil says, motioning everyone to huddle around him. Wlen, still no bigger than a boot, waddles into the middle of the huddle.

"STILL OUT THERE," FOLIT ANNOUNCES, NOT TAKING HIS EYES off the sensor display on his borrowed console.

Zephyr inhales. "Okay." She works the controls, using the maneuvering thrusters to guide the *Ghost* closer to the burnt world below. While detectable, the maneuvering thrusters are far harder to detect than the sub-light engines, especially against the backdrop of a heavily irradiated planet. Unfortunately if they get any closer, gravity will begin pulling them towards the surface.

"Any closer and we're going to start lighting up," Folit says.

Branx looks up from the tactical station. "We could destroy it." He holds up a hand before Zephyr can reply. "I've been studying the passive scan results. It's at best a corvette class vessel. Bigger than us, but this is an Ankarran Raptor."

"Without its crew," Bol Kar points out. Zephyr nods.

"We're not fresh-faced academy graduates," Branx protests. "Look, we don't know its patrol route. It could linger near this planet for days before moving on. If it gets any closer, the decision won't be ours." He continues, "I think we can take it. I've been studying your weapons load out. If we can jam the comms, we should be able to destroy that ship."

"Should?" Folit repeats. "I assume if we are unsuccessful at destroying it, or jamming its comms, this entire thing is for naught?"

Bol Kar nods. "Yeah, this feels risky. Can we try to get around the planet?"

Zephyr shakes her head. "Not on maneuvering thrusters alone. That thing will pick up our sub-light engines almost immediately."

She taps the thumbs of her right hand together. She looks up. "T'Kinlo, what's our status?"

"Your stealth systems are still not one hundred percent. I've replaced a few of the fused relays and emitters, but at best, you'll be hard to spot, not impossible."

"What about comms? Can you boost our jamming capabilities?" There's a pause. Zephyr looks at Sekma, then Branx. Both men shrug. She looks at the ceiling. "T'Kinlo?"

"I'm thinking!" the mutated Trenbal engineer growls. "Okay, yeah. I can do this." The intercom beeps twice.

"I think she hung up on me," Zephyr says.

"She did," Folit agrees.

The intercom beeps. "Okay, go."

Zephyr looks around the bridge. "Uh…"

The intercom growls, "I've rerouted power to the communication system processors and reinforced the transceiver array. Jam away."

"Oh, dren. Well, okay then." Zephyr looks over her shoulder at Sekma, shrugging.

The spiny Sylban man looks at his console and nods, his toothless mouth open in a smile.

Zephyr turns to Branx, hiding her grimace. "Get on it." She pushes a button, bringing main power back online.

Zephyr brings the *Ghost* up and around, leaving the upper atmosphere behind them. The patrol ship is a few million kilometers and closing.

"Sekma?"

"We gotta get closer for the jamming to be completely effective," the computer replies.

Everyone turns to look at the Sylban mutant, who shrugs. The computer says, "It seemed to make sense to have a way to communicate." He shrugs.

Zephyr smiles, then looks at Branx. "Weapons free, bring the noise." The Malkorite man nods, the jewelry on his large ears twinkling and jangling. She catches herself. "But, you know, quietly."

Halfway between the *Ghost* and the patrol ship, Team B is drifting toward the station. Jacoby, clinging near Demfley's head, looks back and makes a hand gesture.

"I think that means we're almost there," Toph offers.

"Or that she's almost out of air," Cynthia replies.

"Cheery," Nellin says. He points. "Look." The station called Naetu is barely visible against the backdrop of space. The docking section at the bottom of the station is a faint yellow light.

"Go!" Wil whispers as the hatch slides open. Breeze fades from sight as she moves first through the hatch. Bennie, carrying Wlen in one hand and his beam saber hilt in the other, goes next, followed by Gabe and Maxim. Wil brings up the rear.

Breeze moves down a meter-long corridor that opens to a T-shaped intersection. To the right, she can see that the corridor opens up. She heads right. She sub-vocalizes into her jury-rigged commset, "It opens up to the right. Two security droids."

Bennie turns left, moving far more quietly than Wil is used to. Maxim and Gabe are trying to be as quiet as they can, so Maxim has the stealth systems on his scout armor at full power. Without the HUD in his own armor, Wil wouldn't be able to tell where the big Palorian is.

"Caretaker is sitting on a sofa," Breeze reports, having made it past the two security droids.

Wil is about to tell everyone to strike, when he trips.

The caretaker, a portly Harrith man, spins. "What was that?" he demands of the two security droids. Both turn and head toward the sound. Blaster bolts lance out, striking both before they can fire their weapons, causing the caretaker to scream. He shifts on the sofa he's perched on, reaching for the arm where a red button is slowly pulsing.

Wil and Maxim round the bend just as the Harrith man's finger stabs at the button, only to stop just short, striking something that ripples slightly at his touch.

"More droids!" Bennie says from the other side of the space. His announcement over the comms is followed by the snap-hiss of his beam saber igniting.

Gabe and Maxim approach the heavyset Harrith man, Maxim returning to visibility. "Hello. We're here to rob you," he says as his mirrored face plate slides up and out of the way.

The man stammers as his finger refuses to move the final few inches to the alarm button. Finally, Breeze shimmers to visibility herself, revealing that the caretaker's finger is pressing against the palm of her long-fingered hand. "Hello," she says, her smile wide, cranial ridges exaggerated by her mutation.

"By the gods!" the man screams, pushing away from her and the alarm button, shifting to the opposite side of the couch that is his command center. "What the wurrin are you?" He screams. "Who are you people?"

Blaster bolts strike the wall over the man's head as Bennie falls back from the opposite side of the space. Three security droids come into view. Breeze drops to a crouch, still protecting the alarm button. Maxim and Gabe return fire as Wil darts back the way they came to flank the droids.

"There's a storage room or something," Bennie says, his beam saber doing its best to intercept blaster bolts but only stopping a few as he moves around the edge of another room off the living space.

"Got it," Wil says. He sees a corridor like the one they came from. Another droid comes out and turns toward him. He barely gets off two shots before it returns fire. One of his shots lands, striking the droid in the shoulder, damaging the arm.

"Would you like some assistance, sir?" Jarvis asks.

"Yes, please," Wil says as he backs toward the corridor they came from, his armor heating up as several of the droid's blaster bolts strike him. His arm suddenly jerks and swings up a few degrees. He squeezes the trigger on his pulse pistol, blasting a hole in the security droid's head.

He gets up as fast as he can and rounds the corner the droid came from just as another is leaving a room at the end of the short corridor. His arm moves on its own, pulled by the powerful servomotors in his armor. He pulls the trigger again as the droid raises its blasters. As the droid collapses, Wil peeks around the edge of the door the droid just came through. Several more are powering up. He grabs two small devices from the belt of his armor, and after pressing small blue buttons at the tops, he tosses them in, grabbing the hatch and slamming it closed. He fires twice at the locking mechanism as a dull thump shakes the bulkhead.

He comes around the corner to find the other two droids on the ground. The caretaker and the rest of the team are gathered around the sofa. Wlen is back to her normal size, standing off to the side with Breeze.

Wil turns to the Harrith man. "Hi there."

# CHAPTER 17_

# GETTING BEAT UP_

THE *GHOST* RATTLES, and sparks erupt from something over the primary display, causing the image on it to waver. The patrol ship fills most of the display, several turrets tracking the smaller *Ghost*.

"I assumed you all knew what you were doing!" T'Kinlo shouts from the intercom.

"Are we still jamming?" Zephyr asks, banking the ship in a tight turn as they pass the patrol ship. They have to stay close to maintain the most effective jamming.

"Yes, but if we're dead, it won't matter." Sekma is clutching the sides of his console as the *Ghost* shakes from incoming fire.

"You said you had this." Zephyr glares at Branx.

"I'm trying, if you could hold us steady," the Malkorite replies, taking a second to wipe his brow.

"You know that's not how this works, right?" the Palorian woman replies, pushing the controls hard over again. The corvette swings past on the display, then returns.

Blaster bolts leap from the engine nacelle-mounted disrupters, while the smaller turret above and behind the bridge also fires. "We have missiles," Zephyr says.

"What?" Branx says, looking over.

"Perhaps we should have practiced this first," Bol Kar quips from Bennie's console. His multitude of arms extend in all directions to keep him stationary.

Folit jumps up to help Branx, his tentacles hastening him over Branx's station to look over the other man's shoulder.

"Can you hear me? Are you dead up there?" T'Kinlo demands.

Zephyr looks up. "Bit busy!" She stabs a control on the arm of her chair, cutting the intercom.

Something near Bennie's station smokes. Bol Kar grunts and starts swatting at a section of the console. "This thing is a death trap!"

"Bring us around!" Folit shouts over the noise.

The patrol ship swings back into view on the primary display, energy bolts leaping from it to strike the *Ghost*'s shields. Two bright flashes leave the bottom of the screen to close the distance between the two ships.

Zephyr pulls the flight controls, bringing the ship away from the patrol ship as the two missiles impact its shields. "Get ready!" she says as she pushes the controls, forcing the *Ghost* into a tight end-over-end twist, bringing the corvette back onto the primary display. Two more missiles leap out, accompanied by a steady stream of blaster bolts. This time the pair of missiles passes through the taxed shields of the patrol ship to rip into its hull. Something somewhere is on fire. Smoke is wafting in from somewhere. Two more missiles finish off the enemy ship.

"Can someone put out the fire?" Zephyr asks as the rapidly expanding debris of the patrol ship clears on the primary display. She looks over her shoulder, "Kill the Jamming."

Sekma makes a noise like he's clearing his throat. The computer asks, "I am getting a signal from the others,"

Zephyr looks over her shoulder, clears her throat, and nods. "Go ahead, Wil."

"You guys doing okay out there? Staying out of the trouble?"

"Sure, all quiet here. You find the arcs?"

"Well, not yet. Are the others on their way? We've secured the control center."

Zephyr nods to herself. "They are. Do you happen to know how many patrol ships there are here in the system?"

There is a pause. "Uh, I'll see what we can find. How many have you seen?" The worry is thick in his voice.

"Just the one so far," she replies.

THE STATIC ATMOSPHERE BARRIER OVER THE ENTRANCE glimmers ahead of Demfley and her passengers.

"See anything?" Cynthia asks.

"Just an old shuttle," Nellin replies, pointing to a small, ancient-looking shuttle pod in the back corner of the docking area. It doesn't look like it's flown anywhere in cycles. "Wait!" He points. Next to a hatch that must lead to lifts is a pair of droids. One looks well-armed; the other looks to have advanced sensors at the ends of its arms.

"Dren," Toph curses.

Nellin pulls a rifle from the magnetic attachment on his back, shifting to move the heavy blanket away from him.

Jacoby waves to get their attention, making a series of hand gestures and motions. Demfley convulses, causing everyone to look at the turtle-shaped being. Jacoby points to her and nods.

"I think she's running out of air," Cynthia says.

Toph points to Jacoby. "I thought they didn't need air?"

Cynthia shakes her head. "They do, just not as much as us, and they can go without, but not forever."

"If everyone could shut up and let me focus..." Nellin raises the rifle to the faceplate of his environment suit. He centers his scope on the security droid and pulls the trigger. The bolt of supercharged plasma leaps from the barrel of the rifle to pass through the static atmosphere barrier and enter the head of the droid, ripping part of it clear of the body.

The sensor droid turns to the hatch, moving to open it until its head also explodes. The body falls to the floor.

Demfley shudders as she seems to muster a last burst of air from her rear flippers. They drift toward the energy barrier.

## BRASS TACKS_

"I'll wait here," Demfley says. They've carried her behind the shuttle pod in the back corner of the landing bay. She's been wheezing since they passed through the atmospheric barrier, taking deep gulps of air.

Jacoby smiles as best his physiology allows. "Stay safe. We'll be back for you."

Cynthia looks at her wristcomm. "There's a wireless network, but it's heavily encrypted."

"Can you raise your Captain?" Toph asks, slipping out of her environment suit.

Cynthia shakes her head. "We don't know what's up here. A comm could attract attention we don't want."

Jacoby turns a slow circle. "So...what? We wait here?"

"Captain, the others have arrived," Gabe says. He is standing next to the wall-mounted display in front of the caretaker's sofa.

Wil looks into the bedroom they are keeping the caretaker in. "Sit tight." He nods to Maxim, who is standing at the door, guarding it. "Can you open a channel that won't attract the rest of the security droids?"

Bennie walks out of the head. "I wouldn't go in there."

Wil makes a face, then turns to Gabe, who says, "Unfortunately, no. We have full control of the external systems of this station, but it appears that the Consortium sought safeguards wherever possible." Data tendrils withdraw from the frame of the wall display. He turns to Bennie. "Have you found anything?"

Bennie is sitting on the sofa next to the arm embedded with the alert button and several other controls. He looks up from his wrist-comm. "Nothing. The droids all operate on a separate system. The ones up here were based in that room." He looks at Wil. "Perhaps if their room wasn't destroyed..." Wil flips him off. "The other depot is the level above the docking bay."

Wlen waddles over. "I can go get them." She points to the bank of lifts in the center of the control center. "Those must run the length of the station. One assumes the caretaker has free run of the station."

Wil looks at Maxim, who leans into the bedroom. "Hey, can you move about this place freely?" The caretaker says something Wil and the others can't understand. Maxim nods.

Wil turns to Wlen. "Okay, go." She nods, tentacles quivering as she moves on stubby legs toward the lift.

Wil enters the bedroom. "So, we're looking for something." He smiles his most disarming smile. "We're hoping you can help us find it."

"Wha—what are you looking for? I don't know wha-what's kept here."

Wil smiles. "In this case, we think you might."

The man wrings his hands. "We don't get to know. That's how this works. The droids police me, I monitor the systems. The droids have no access to the internex, and I have no access to the inventory." He starts to weep, burying his face in his hands. "I don't want to die."

"Oh, come on, man," Maxim groans. "Don't start crying."

Wil rubs his face. "What about Consortium goods?"

The man looks up. "Con-Consortium goods? You're robbing th-them?" He snuffles.

"This is just not dignified," Maxim moans, turning to leave the room.

Wil kneels down to face the man. "We're not going to hurt you. We're looking for a few data archives. That's it."

The caretaker looks up. "Data arcs?" Wil nods. "Consortium goods are stored in arm one. There's a storage unit there, twice the size of the rest." He looks Wil in the eye. "You have to take me with you. They'll kill me."

Wil bites his lip, "Yeah, we can take you with us, drop you somewhere they won't find you." The caretaker nods, snuffling. Wil adds, "Oh yeah, how many patrol ships are in the system? Do you know their routes?"

"Patrol ships?" The caretaker looks past Wil. "I didn't know there were any. They must only report in if there's a problem."

Wil sighs. "Of course."

"Well, we can't just stand here all day...or is night? Whatever, we have to do something," Nellin argues, again.

Cynthia nods. "I know, but we don't know what's going on yet. We could open that hatch and be face to face with more security droids."

Before anyone can say anything, the hatch they are arguing about opens. Wlen is standing there. "You ready?" she asks.

# LET'S DO THIS_

"Glad you're alive," Cynthia says as she exits the lift in the control center at the top of the station. She hugs Wil the best she can with both of them in combat armor.

"Very sweet," Jarvis says.

Wil ignores the AI. "Love seeing you." He looks past Cynthia. "All of you. We know where to go. Some of us need to stay here and keep an eye on the caretaker and make sure no one calls or anything." He's about to pick a few people when Nellin raises his hand.

"Toph can stay up here," the big Tygran man says.

Wil tries to hide his surprise, though his eyebrows are as high as they can get. He shrugs. "Okay." He points to the door Maxim is standing outside of. "He's in there. We did a sweep and removed or disabled any comm gear." He points to the sofa the large group is now congregating next to. "We also disabled the alarm button in the sofa."

"Droids?" Toph asks.

Bennie shakes his head. "All the ones on this level are disabled or destroyed." He adds, "The rest are either patrolling the four storage areas or in a depot just above the docking area."

Breeze raises her hand. "I'll stay here, too. I don't imagine a need for flying or turning invisible, especially with droids."

Maxim nods. "I thought droids couldn't see you?"

She tilts her head. "It takes a lot out of me to get that insubstantial."

He nods again, tilting his head to one side. "Makes sense."

Wlen moves to stand next to her much taller friend. "I'll stay here, too. I think we'll be in the way down there, especially if things get hairy." She looks around. "Plus, I'm exhausted having stayed so large for so long. I could use a nap." Wil nods.

Bennie looks down at his screen. "I think I can take care of the droid problem. Gimmie a microtock." He focuses on the screen on his wrist.

"I'll still stay here," Breeze says, hugging her arms around herself.

Toph walks over to Bennie. "How are you hacking them?" She moves to look at his wristcomm screen.

Bennie glances up. "I'm flooding the wireless network with junk data and embedding a subroutine that should send them all to the depot to run a diagnostic." He looks at the Olop woman. "Boom, done." He looks at Wil. "That should buy us a tock, at least."

Wil looks around. "Okay, let's do this." He moves to the bank of lifts, pressing the call button. Everyone moves closer to the lifts. The doors part, and as everyone files in, Wil says, "Lock and load. We don't know where the other droids are."

NEWSCAST_



"This is GNO News Break. I'm Mon-El Furash. I'm aboard the Peacekeeper Command Carrier *Pax Imperious*. We're en route to, well... I don't actually know. Our destination is being kept secret, but I'm told another group of the mysterious warships has been sighted."

Back in the studio, someone asks a question.

Furash nods, her numerous earrings jingling. "That's right, the battle near the Void ended in what can best be described as a draw. The unknown attackers withdrew but did do more damage than the Peacekeepers. Why they withdrew is still unknown." She listens. "Captain Benesch tells me the *Pax Imperious* will take a fleet command role when we arrive wherever we're going, so I should be relatively safe."

She shakes her head. "Unfortunately no, Belzar. The identity of these attackers is still unknown. They have yet to answer any hails, and no survivors that I know of have been captured."

# PART FIVE

# CHAPTER 18_

## YOU JUST NEVER KNOW_

BREEZE IS STANDING in the doorway to the caretaker's living quarters while Toph busies herself somewhere else. They found an equipment room that the small Olop woman wants to investigate. Wlen is lying on the sofa trying to regain her energy after carrying the boarding team inside her throat pouch for so long.

"Who are you people? What are you?" the caretaker asks from the bed he's sitting on.

"I'm Palorian," Breeze replies, "though you'd never know from looking at me." She smiles as she raises her right arm, the thin membrane unfolding between her long fingers and stretching to her side. As she retracts her wing membrane, she turns invisible.

"Neat," the Harrith man exhales, watching the display.

Breeze smiles sadly. "Just a few side effects."

The man nods. "And what? You're stealing the means to make more of you or something? What's the Consortium have to do with this? Do they have a cure?" He looks at the floor. "Stealing from them is a death sentence."

Breeze shrugs. "I don't imagine I have a lot of time, anyway. I'm a genetic mutant created from unstable, unknowable DNA from a creature not of this galaxy." She shrugs again. "Such is life."

The caretaker is about to answer when the lights go out.

"What the—" Breeze says as the muffled sound of a blaster firing rings throughout the control center. She immediately turns invisible, hissing, "Stay here." She creeps toward the living space where Wlen was napping on the sofa. She finds her friend's body still on the sofa.

"Come on out, there's only one way this ends," Toph shouts from somewhere in the space. Breeze can't see anything in the nearly pitch-black space. She's hoping Toph can't see anything, either.

"What's going on?" the caretaker shouts, then screams as another blaster bolt is fired, briefly illuminating the space. Breeze sees the small special operations member standing next to the caretaker's body at the door to the bedroom.

"I know you're here somewhere, freak," Toph says. Her voice is more distant. She must be heading back to the equipment room. Breeze heads off in the opposite direction, past the sofa and the restroom and the droid storage room, knowing she'll come around to the far side of the circular space and the equipment room.

As she circles around to the short corridor leading to the door of the equipment room, she hears Toph whisper, "You might be invisible, but you don't have the energy to mask your body heat yet." The next and last thing she hears is the firing of a pulse pistol.

Toph taps a control on her wristcomm, turning the lights in the control center back on. She holsters her pistol and walks into the equipment room, sliding a pair of goggles into a pouch on her hip.

Racks of equipment line the room, fans whirring away to keep things cool. Despite the Consortium's clear distrust of their underlings, someone carefully labeled each piece of equipment in the room. She walks to the rack of equipment labeled "Communications" and types a few commands in. Then she looks around and finds "Droid Management" and gets to work. She plugs a wire into her wristcomm. She accesses a program and uploads new instructions.

She disconnects from the racks of equipment and heads for the bay of lifts in the center of the circular living space. The doors to one of the lift cars slide open, and she walks in, humming a song to herself.

# WHO TO TRUST_

THE LIFT DOORS SLIDE APART. Several pulse pistol barrels stick out. Wil leans out, looking left and right. "No droids."

Bennie shoves him out of the lift car. "Then go. It's crowded in here."

Wil spins. "Little asshole." Bennie exits the lift car, waving Wil's insult aside. Everyone else follows him.

Gabe makes a slow circle. "I am detecting no other droids on this deck. The storage areas are empty." He gestures around the circular space to the four large hatches evenly spaced around the central column.

Cynthia says, "We should close all the hatches. If the droids come back, they'll have to figure out which one we're in."

Nellin nods. "Good call." He turns to Jacoby, who nods. They both head off to one of the storage areas.

Wil looks at the others, then at the hatch to the storage module the Consortium keeps their cargo module loot crate in. "Let's get those arcs. We can call in the *Ghost* and get the hell out of here."

Walking into the storage area, Wil looks around and points at a storage module that's easily three times the size of the rest in the large rectangular space. It is clearly not a removable module. "That's it. Gabe, can you and Bennie get those doors open?"

The hacker and droid move to the pair of large doors. They work for a few minutes, muttering to each other. Wil looks at Cynthia, who shrugs, smiling. With a series of clunks, the front of the module splits and two heavy doors swing open, segmenting to open like an accordion.

Wil peers around the door nearest him as it swings past. "Huh."

Maxim looks over at him. "You just played some dramatic music in your head, huh?" He looks into the now open module. "Oh."

Wil nods. "Yeah, and right?" Shelves line the walls of the large storage module, each loaded with tanks of liquid and computing cores.

And droids.

One of them, a design similar to Len, turns. "You are not authorized to be here."

Another turns. "I will alert security." It tilts its head. "They have corrupted the network."

A third turns to block a floor-to-ceiling tank with some kind of chitin-armored, embryo-like creature inside it. "Protocol seven."

Wil looks at Maxim. The others have gathered behind them. "Protocol seven?" The three droids are joined by two more. As a group, their optic sensors turn red as modified pulse pistols slide up and over their shoulders on short, articulated mounts.

"Protocol seven," Maxim says as he shoves Wil out of the way, diving to the side. The others follow suit. Super charge plasma flies out of the module, scoring the wall opposite.

Cynthia ducks and returns fire. Gabe shifts into combat mode and engages. The research droids move quickly, ducking behind equipment. They are remarkably nimble for research models. The return fire is shredding equipment and bio tanks alike.

Two of the droids leap out of the modified storage module, firing in all directions. Gabe destroys one mid-leap while the other lands on Maxim, driving him to the ground.

Bennie's beam saber ignites. "I got you, big guy!" He leaps into the air, readying a slice that will cut the attacking droid in half, only to get stopped mid-air by said droid's foot as it lashes out with a kick that sends Bennie toward the main hatch connecting the storage area to the main hub of the station. Definitely upgraded from standard scientific research models.

Nellin races back from the main section of the station, his two pistols barking as high energy plasma leaps from them. He moves to where Wil is taking cover.

"Think Len can do this stuff?" Wil asks, crouching to avoid a volley of energy blasts. The storage area has little to offer in the way of cover.

"That's what's on your mind right now?" Nellin shouts as he fires, clipping one of the droids still in the lab on the shoulder, driving it behind a computer processing core that is already riddled with scorch marks.

Wil rolls toward the lab, firing on the same droid, striking the computer core twice and the droid twice in the head. He looks at the big Tygran man. "That and what we should eat for dinner when we're done here." He winks and rushes into the lab module to take out the last droid inside.

The droid attacking Maxim falls to the ground in a metallic clatter, an energy blade sticking out of the back of its head. Cynthia is standing over it. She helps Maxim up. His armor has several new dents.

Wil looks around. "Do we know what the data archives look like?" He rests a hand on the computing core he shot up. "Hopefully not like this."

Maxim walks in and goes to the back corner of the module, a place few energy bolts landed. "Got 'em," he says.

"Are they—" Cynthia starts.

"Intact? Yeah," the big man says.

Wil comes around the corner as Gabe joins them. The droid confirms, "Those are the archives." He points to the Farsight Corporation logo on both of them. Each is roughly a two-foot by three-foot rectangle. There are status lights on the narrow end and a display on the long side with data connection ports next to it.

Wil reaches out to grab one of the archives, tugging on it. He grunts, letting go. He looks at Gabe and Maxim. "Why don't you two grab them?"

Maxim tuts, pushing past Wil, who walks back out of the module. "Time to go."

Nellin looks around. "That's it?"

Cynthia looks at him. "Unless you want a souvenir." She hitches a thumb over her shoulder into the mostly ruined lab module. A piece of something falls off a shelf, clattering to the deck.

The Tygran special operations agent looks around. "Then, I guess we're done here." He checks his wristcomm and smiles. "Yeah, guess we're done."

Wil tilts his head. "Well, yeah, that's what Maxim just said."

Maxim nods. "Yeah."

Gabe, still standing near the lab module, spins toward the open hatch connecting to the main station facility. What must be every remaining functional droid on the station rushes from the service lift set in the wall and the main lift. Security droids have their weapons raised, and sensor droids are standing in front of them as moving shields.

Wil looks at his mechanical friend, then the droids, then Nellin. "You son of a bitch. You sold us out?"

ZEPHYR and her mismatched crew have been sitting a few million kilometers from the station, waiting for word from their friends. They have encountered no other patrols and T'Kinlo has gotten most of the damage repaired during the wait.

"A signal is coming in. It is being broadcast from the station," the computer says for Sekma.

Zephyr turns to look over her shoulder at the Sylban, catching Branx check his wristcomm as she does. She looks at the Malkorite, about to ask if he knows what the signal is, when he draws a pulse pistol, firing a single shot into the back Bol Kar's head. The spider-like legs of the now dead, previously Malkorite man spasm, slapping controls. Several alarms go off as the tactical station receives input.

"What the—" Zephyr says as Branx coolly turns and fires across the bridge at Folit. It takes several shots. Many strike the various displays that Bennie has mounted to his console. Sparks and smoke erupt from the ruined equipment as Folit slumps in his chair, tentacles dangling limply.

Zephyr raises a small, clear cover and slaps a square red button on the edge of the console. A button that Gabe installed after Lorath took over the ship a few cycles ago. As the button lights up at her touch, she slithers out of the chair into the space between the chair and command console, just as a plasma blast strikes the back of the chair. "Sekma! Down!" she shouts as she draws her own pulse pistol, leaning around the front of the console to return fire. She hears the bridge hatch open and looks. Sekma is holding the hatch open from behind, his face peeking out from behind it.

"Branx! What are you doing?" she shouts as she crawls toward the back of the bridge, doing her best to keep the command and pilot station between her and Branx as best she can. She fires a few bolts into the bulkhead opposite her to encourage her foe to not come this way.

She gets as close to the hatch as possible. Several blaster bolts strike the rear bulkhead and the hatch itself, forcing Sekma to move his head back from the hatch. Zephyr stands, firing twice in the direction the previous energy bolts just came from, dashing through the hatch. "Close it, close it!" Several more blasts strike the hatch and frame before the sound of the heavy hatch slamming closed reaches her ears. She rolls over to see the worried thorny Sylban man looking down at her. He moves to offer her a hand up but realizes dangerous-looking spines protrude from his palm and knuckles. He shrugs and takes a step back to give Zephyr room to stand.

"What the wurrin?" she asks as she presses a control set next to the hatch. Several metallic clunks boom from inside the door. "He's locked in."

The tree-like man looks at her, then the hatch, making a series of hand gestures that Zephyr doesn't understand. "Yeah, I don't know what you're saying, but at a guess, no, it's not good that he's locked on the bridge." She turns to head down the long corridor connecting the forward section of the *Ghost* to the much larger aft section. "Come on, let's get to engineering."

As they pass through the common area, Sekma makes another round of indecipherable hand gestures. When Zephyr shrugs, he makes a button pushing motion.

"Ah! Why didn't you just say that?" She meets his eye. "Sorry.

That button was an emergency disconnect of primary bridge functions." She shakes her head as the first set of doors slides apart, revealing the short corridor with the medbay on one side and computer core on the other. At the end, the hatch to engineering. "This isn't the first time hostile *forces* have taken the *Ghost*. Gabe installed it a while back." She changes her voice a bit to sound like her mechanical friend. "Just in case."

The doors to engineering slide apart. "Dren!" Zephyr hisses. T'Kinlo is lying in a pool of orange blood. She ushers Sekma into the engineering space. "Branx is good." When the doors slide closed, she presses a control next to the frame, locking the doors. She looks around. "Where is Len?"

## BETRAYAL_

Maxim places his pistols on top of the pile of weapons next to the lift bank. He looks up at Nellin. "You suck."

The Tygran man shrugs, motioning for Maxim to back up with the others. He turns to Gabe. "I know you're fast enough to take me out, but Toph instructed these droids to kill everyone before focusing their efforts on you. You'll probably be the last one standing, but I'm pretty sure that isn't a win in your book." He smirks.

Gabe says nothing, his eyes flash from their normal yellow to red, then back again.

The lift doors slide apart and Toph walks over. "Signal sent, sir."

Nellin nods. "Go find the bug guy." He waves off across the central column. "I think he went into area three, last I saw. Maybe he closed himself inside?"

She nods. "What's he do? Invisible, too? Wings under his carapace? Spits acid?"

Nellin looks at Wil, who shrugs. "Ballon animals. He's freaky good at it. They extrude out of his... well..." He grins. "Or maybe he turns into an actual beetle? It's hard to keep these things straight. Spitting acid, beetles, who knows?"

Nellin turns to Toph. "Find him, shoot to kill." She nods and takes off across the central column space.

Toph walks into the storage area, pulse pistol held at the ready. "Come out, come out, wherever you are." She looks around the space. Nothing. She walks to the pedestal, checking it. Nothing.

She turns to exit the massive rectangular storage area when two large clawed hands reach down from above, one clamping over her mouth. Sinewy fibrous tissue retracts between forearm and upper arm chitin. Jacoby's body had long ago given up having bones in favor of his thick exoskeleton. The arms pull her up halfway to the ceiling until she's face to face with Jacoby. As she flails, she tries to bring her pistol to bare. His smaller arms reach out, grasping her arms. His eyeless face regards her as his mandible jaws open and close. "I can extend my limbs," he whispers before biting into her neck, killing her, spilling her lifeblood all over himself and the deck below.

As her body twitches its last, her finger convulses on the trigger. The pistol barks once before her body goes slack, her grip on the pulse pistol releasing. The gun hits the ground with a clatter.

Back in the storage area, several droids spin at the sound of the pistol blast. So does Nellin, he smiles at his prisoners, tail swishing languidly.

Wil looks at Gabe, nodding slowly. Nellin took their guns, and Bennie's beam saber, but has no idea what Wil's armor is capable of. He raises both hands, palms out.

The same moment super charged plasma leaps from his hands into several of the nearest security droids, Gabe drops to a crouch, switching to combat mode quickly. He opens fire from both forearm blasters.

"Dren!" Nellin hisses, backing towards cover. He looks at two droids, "Grab the archives!"

"Cover!" Wil shouts, stepping sideways as his palm-mounted plasma blasters keep up their fire.

"Sir, the palm units are overheating."

Wil moves towards their confiscated guns.

Bennie is behind him until he's close enough to dart out from around Wil, diving to grab his beam saber hilt.

The security droids immediately grab scanner droids to use as shields as they bring their weapons around.

Bennie leaps towards a pair of security droids, his beam saber swinging in a bright blue arc. He intercepts a few energy bolts as he covers the distance, dodging the others. Three slashes leave the droids without legs, one without an arm, and then both without their heads. He doesn't slow down as he grabs one of the torsos, holding it up to deflect several incoming energy bolts.

"Wil!" Maxim shouts. Wil kicks a pistol towards his friend, then sees Cynthia and kicks a pistol to her as a blast strikes his shoulder, eliciting a grunt as he drops to a knee. His armor is smoking where the blaster bolt struck it.

Maxim grabs a pistol as he falls back toward the still open Consortium cargo module. Cynthia is with him, laying down cover fire.

Nellin and the remaining droids fall back into the central column as Wil and the team take cover behind the Consortium cargo module's doors. Nellin reaches for something on the side of the hatch.

The hatch connecting the storage area to the central column slams shut. Wil walks over to it. He slams a fist against it. "Damnit!"

Cynthia joins him. "That drennog."

Maxim turns to Bennie. "They can't call for help, right?"

The Brailack shakes his head. "I'm certain they can. Toph had access to the equipment upstairs. There must be a comm node. She also saw my hack and likely understands how to undo it."

Wil grimaces, pointing to the door. "Get this open." Bennie nods.

"What do you think happened to Breeze and Wlen?" Cynthia asks.

Maxim makes a noise. "I'm guessing they're dead." He looks at Wil. "It's a fair bet that Branx is in on this, too. If Toph sent a signal, he got it, and our friends on the ship are in trouble."

Wil frowns. "Damn. Good point."

"Dren!" Bennie hisses. "Gabe, I need your help!"

Gabe rushes to his side. Wil follows. "What's wrong?"

"They're trying to eject us."

Wil's eyes go wide. "They can do that?"

"So it would seem," Gabe offers, extending data tendrils into the side of the hatch controls, careful to not crowd Bennie, who has a data cable strung from his wristcomm to a splice he's attached to a wire under the panel.

Wil spins in a slow circle, taking in the rectangular storage area, finally stopping at Bennie and Gabe. "Can you stop them?"

Bennie looks up from his wristcomm. "Maybe. Shut up."

# RETURN TO SENDER_

"Tʜᴇʏ ᴍᴜsᴛ ʙᴇ in the cargo hold," Zephyr says to herself. She looks around, realizing that over the cycles she has spent little time in the engine room. Finding the comm panel, she presses a few buttons. "Len? Can you read me? Come in, Len."

Silence.

Sekma raps a wood-like knuckle on a control console to get Zephyr's attention. When she turns, he points to something.

Zephyr walks back to him and looks down. "Dren. He's trying to bypass navigation." She watches the display for a beat. "And making excellent progress." She taps a few commands into the console. "That should slow him down."

She moves to reach past Sekma, catching her jumpsuit sleeve on one of his thorns. She looks up. "Excuse me." He shuffles back, reaching up to rub his neck. She works at a console, then says for his benefit, "Okay, I've done what I can. Let's go get Len and retake the bridge." She turns to the Sylban man. His bark-like skin is matte black and looks like a mix of tree bark and insect exoskeleton, interspersed with wicked looking thorns.

They leave engineering, and as they pass the hatch to the

medbay, the door slides open. Zephyr collides with Len as they step out into the corridor.

"Oh, excuse me!" the research droid exclaims, raising their arms and stepping back.

"Len! Glad we found you," Zephyr says, Sekma nodding vigorously behind her.

"Oh, why? Is someone injured?" The research droid turns to look at the two unoccupied bio beds.

"No. Well, yes, but they're dead," Zephyr answers, pushing the droid into medbay.

"Oh, my."

"We're it. Branx killed Folit, Bol Kar, and T'Kinlo."

"To what end?"

"Being a bad guy, that's what they do." Zephyr peeks back into the short corridor. "Let's go."

"Go where? Should we not hide and wait for the others?"

"They're probably in worse trouble than we are," Zephyr counters. Again, Sekma nods his agreement.

"I see. I am not a combat droid," Len says, then tilts their head, "but will do what I can to help." They gesture out into the corridor. "Lead the way."

Part of the anti-takeover protocols Gabe installed included disabling all internal sensors. The *Ghost*'s systems are not advanced enough to allow the crew to have access while keeping boarders out of the system. Everyone is equally blind.

They enter the armory below the bridge. Zephyr walks over to her alcove, reaching for the chest piece of her Peacekeeper scout armor. "Grab what you want," she says, slipping out of her jumpsuit. Sekma moves around the small armory like he's browsing the selection at a food stall. Len is still standing in the entry. He scans the room slowly, then reaches out, removing two fist-sized cylinders from a rack.

Sekma reaches for a heavy baton in Maxim's alcove.

Zephyr finishes getting dressed, clicking the gauntlet on her left forearm closed over her wristcomm. The computing device lights up as her armor systems integrate with it. As she secures her helmet over her head, the HUD activates, all systems green. "Let's go."

The hatch outside the bridge still shows a blinking red icon. Zephyr looks at the others. "He's still in there. I don't know where he'll be, but likely Wil's seat. That console has full access to all ship's systems. I'll open the hatch and rush in, going low. My armor will render me invisible."

She gestures to the sides of the hatch. "You two stay on either side. You'll know if I need you."

Sekma nods. Len's optic sensors rotate.

Zephyr taps a code into the control panel next to the bridge hatch. The icon turns green as she taps her wristcomm. She pulls the hatch open as she vanishes from sight. Her two cohorts move to the side of the hatch as blaster bolts fly through the open hatch.

Zephyr moves quickly. Branx is standing in front of Wil's console, several panels opened to expose the wiring and circuitry inside. He has his pistol aimed at the hatch still, watching. A metallic arm shows itself tossing a canister into the bridge. Branx fires, blowing the arm to pieces.

Zephyr moves as the canister fills the bridge with smoke. She tackles the Malkorite special operations agent, driving him to the ground. She knocks the pistol from his hand as he tries to bring it to bear under her. He's able to get a foot under her, shoving her off of him, into the side of Cynthia's station. He gets to his feet fast, a knife now in his hand.

Zephyr disengages the cloaking systems in her armor and retracts her mirrored faceplate. "You're going to pay for this."

"Your friends are dead. Why not stand down? We can make it worth your while." He lunges.

Zephyr lets the blade strike her midsection. It glances off the armor plating as she reaches out to grab Branx's ears. He screams. She pulls his head down as she drives her knee up. The cartilage of his ears snaps from the force. "Clear," she shouts as the unconscious Malkorite falls to the deck with a thud.

She points to Sekma, then the unconscious Branx. "Can you get him to the brig?"

"I will assist," Len says. They turn to reach for the insensate hijacker with their remaining arm, then look at Sekma. "Where is the brig?" Sekma shrugs.

# CHAPTER 19_

# NO PRESSURE_

"Bennie?" Wil presses.

"Shut up," the Brailack hacker replies.

A yellow light begins to strobe from the ceiling.

"Uh, Gabe? Bennie?" Cynthia presses.

Gabe turns from Bennie and walks to the hatch, his right arm shifting, whirs and clicks punctuating the silence. A bright beam of super-heated plasma leaps out as he moves the newly created device to the hatch.

"Gabe?" Maxim asks.

"While Bennie works to block their efforts electronically, I have another idea."

Cynthia nods. "They can't jettison if we breach the hatch."

"Correct." Gabe inclines his head. "The automated system likely was not updated to factor in this station's unique purpose. Any breach will lock down the separation protocols." He turns his attention back to the several-inches-long gash he has carved in the first layer of the hatch. He says, lower, "I hope."

"You hope?" Wil repeats.

"Got 'em," Bennie says. He looks up at Gabe. "Good thinking."

He moves to join Gabe, igniting his beam saber. He looks over to Wil. "We'll have to cut our way through. They killed the hatch controls."

Molten metal dribbles down the hatch surface as Bennie's bright blue blade slowly slices through it toward the arc Gabe is cutting.

Maxim looks at Cynthia. "Did you catch how many droids were left?"

She shakes her head. "No, but it couldn't be more than ten."

Gabe looks over his shoulder. "In fact, there are eleven remaining." He turns his attention back to his cutting.

Maxim looks at the hatch. "They're either standing on the other side, ready to fire..."

"...Or they're not there," Cynthia finishes the thought.

"Captain, Wil. Come in." Zephyr's voice comes from the speakers in Wil's armor, causing him to jump.

He raises his arm. "Zee, you're alive. Everything okay? Where are you?"

"We're fine. Mostly. Branx killed Bol Kar, Folit, and T'Kinlo. He almost got the rest of us."

"You got him?" Maxim asks, leaning down to speak into Wil's chest. Wil swats him away.

"We did. He's in the brig. We're coming in now, it's dicey. The heat and radiation is, well, a lot. Have you found the archives?"

Wil looks around. "Technically, yes."

Zephyr's sigh is audible over the comms. "What do you need us to do?"

"Sit tight for now," Wil says. "Get the *Ghost* in the bay and keep her ready."

Cynthia adds, "Oh, get Demfley. She's hiding out behind that old shuttle in the back of the docking bay."

"Copy that," Zephyr replies.

"Hey, Zee!" Bennie rushes over to shout at Wil's chest. "Can the *Ghost*'s sensors pick up the droids, Nellin, and Toph?"

Wil nods to the Brailack hacker. "Good call."

There is a brief pause, then Zephyr replies, "Hard to be certain, but I don't think anyone is on your level. Wait one," She says. In the background, there are some scuffling sounds and grunting. "No, no. Yes, that one. Okay, I'm back. I've got a few droids in the cargo bay. Look like security models."

Wil rubs his chin. "Okay, stick to the plan, but come in slow, like maybe you don't know how to pilot the ship. Don't open up the hatch and be ready."

"Copy." The channel closes.

Wil nods to Gabe, who kicks the section of the hatch he and Bennie have cut through. The metal clangs as it lands a few feet from the hole. The edges are still glowing a faint orange.

Cynthia dives through, rolling to her knees, pistol held at the ready, scanning the room. "Clear."

Bennie follows her, executing a nearly perfect roll before getting to his feet, beam saber igniting.

Wil leans down to look through the hole. "Show offs." He moves to squeeze through the hole.

"Careful, sir. The edges are still quite hot," Jarvis warns.

Wil tuts, "Yes, Mom."

Maxim chuckles as he shoves Wil through the hole. When Wil gets to his feet, he looks around. "Think they killed Jacoby?"

"They didn't," a voice says from across the central column space. Jacoby drops from somewhere above. "Toph is no longer a problem," he says, nearing the others. Her dried blood still covers his arms, torso and mandibles.

Wil makes a face, turning away. "Gross." He mumbles.

"Good to see you breathing," Maxim says, inclining his head. The other man returns the gesture.

"You got Toph?" Cynthia asks. She gestures to the gore covering him.

Jacoby nods. "She's dead. I was going to try to get Nellin, but he's got those droids set up as body guards. I hid."

"How'd you get up there?" Bennie asks.

Jacoby's split mandible mouth does its best to smile. He reaches up toward the ceiling with one hand, and his forearm stretches up into the darkness above. The sinewy flesh under his chitinous exoskeleton segments stretches taut.

"That's gross," Maxim says. Bennie nods, offering a small green fist for his larger bluish friend to bump.

As Jacoby's arm retracts, the flesh making an odd noise, he looks around. "He and his mechanical friends went to the cargo bay."

"We know." Wil grins.

# NEXT STEPS_

"The arcs?" Wil asks.

Jacoby holds his hands about three feet apart. "This big?" Maxim nods. "Took 'em with them."

Wil curses under his breath. He looks around.

Maxim says, "The lifts will be a kill box."

Cynthia nods her agreement but adds, "Unless we can cause a distraction."

Wil rubs his chin. He opens his mouth to say something when the lighting in the central column turns red and pulses. An alert siren comes to life. He looks around. "Is that what I think it is?"

"Guess that means Nellin didn't sell us out to the Consortium," Cynthia says.

"Covering his tracks. They'll think all of us are dead," Maxim adds.

Wil nods.

"Now what?" Bennie asks.

"I'm thinking," Wil snaps.

"Don't hurt yourself," the Brailack snaps back.

Cynthia turns to Bennie. "Can you override the lifts?"

Bennie nods. "Yeah. Why?"

She looks around. "Move the lift cars up to the control center, and open all the shaft doors."

Bennie smiles. "Okay, gimmie a microtock."

Wil looks at her, smiling. He looks at his wristcomm. "Zee, you there?"

"Yup, we're pulling into the cargo bay now. Nellin and a bunch of droids are waiting for us, I sent a text message saying the hull needs to cool, should buy some time." the first officer of the *Ghost* reports.

"Yeah, we're gonna take care of that. Land as far from them as you can and drop the boarding ramp. Keep the cargo doors closed."

"Copy that," Zephyr replies.

Wil looks at Cynthia, then the others. "Everyone get what we're doing?"

"No, not in the slightest," Jacoby says, looking around the group, his segmented mandible jaws slack.

Maxim puts a hand on the big bug-like man. "You're new. Zee is going to do her best to lure Nellin and the bots toward the *Ghost*, away from the lifts. We're going to drop down the shaft and rush them." He grins. "Easy."

"You people are insane," Jacoby says, chitin-armored shoulders slumping.

"Yeah," Bennie agrees, moving his beam saber hilt from hand to hand nervously. He looks to Wil. "Lifts are up at the top and the doors will open on my command."

Wil nods. "Okay, let's do this. This place could blow any minute." He walks over to one of the lift shafts, joined by Maxim and Cynthia. Bennie and Jacoby go to the other set of lift doors. Bennie climbs up onto Jacoby's back. Gabe moves next to the hybrid man.

Wil nods to the Brailack hacker, who returns the gesture and taps his wristcomm. "The cargo bay lift doors will open in twenty milli-tocks." The doors behind them open. Without a word, Jacoby steps into the void, dropping from sight.

Wil looks at the others. "Off we go." He steps into the shaft, dropping. Cynthia and Maxim follow.

## ACTION!_

"THEY ARE COMING CLOSER," the computer announces for Sekma. He's back at the communications console after explaining he had zero weapons or starship training and would likely be a liability at the tactical station.

Zephyr nods. On the main display, she's watching Nellin and eleven security droids move toward the ship. He's called twice, and she's ignored the comms, hoping he assumes that the communications system was damaged by the extreme heat and radiation experienced on approach. The lowered boarding ramp is inviting enough. The *Ghost* is positioned as best she can get it to keep the cargo doors out of sight and keep the ship as far from the wall with the lifts as possible.

As Nellin nears the lowered cargo ramp, the lift doors opposite the cargo bay open. Gabe launches out of the lift shaft, banking sharply to the rear of the space to ensure any fire directed at him doesn't strike his friends as they leave the lift shafts. Jacoby, with Bennie still on his back, hits the deck and heads right toward the collected droids. He reaches his arms up. His sinewy flesh extends so he can grasp an exposed conduit along the ceiling. As he rises, swinging toward the now firing droids, Bennie ignites his beam saber as he leaps from Jacoby's back.

Wil, Maxim, and Cynthia emerge from their shaft, heading toward the wide opening the *Ghost* has come through. Each is angling slightly off of each other's path, making friendly fire less likely.

Every droid turns toward the biological crew of the *Ghost,* remembering their programming to leave Gabe for last. While it made sense earlier, it now leaves Gabe free to strafe the clustered security droids, destroying three of them immediately.

Bennie lands in a crouch, his saber held behind him. As he stands, a security droid draws on him, firing super charged plasma, which Bennie deflects or absorbs on his blade, mostly. Two bolts strike glancing blows on his armor, heating it and pushing him backwards. Getting his feet back under him he dashes toward the droid, driving his blade straight through its torso.

Jacoby lands on the port engine nacelle of the *Ghost* and immediately extends his arms to grasp one of the destroyed droids, using it to bash another into the deck.

Wil, Maxim, and Cynthia continue running and firing as they fan out along the curved wall created by the static atmosphere barrier at the front of the bay. Cynthia, being the fastest, even in armor, runs almost all the way around to the front of the *Ghost,* firing on a droid that is holding one of the data archives. The device clatters to the deck as Nellin pulls the body of the droid in front of him as Cynthia fires twice.

Nellin raises his own pistol to fire on Cynthia, who has nowhere to go for cover, when a bright blue beam of light slices through the gun, the severed half falling to the deck with a thud, sparks erupting from it, and the other half still clutched in Nellin's hand. He jerks around, dodging just in time to avoid a blade swipe that would have removed his hand.

"You little..." Nellin growls, fully turning to Bennie.

Bennie grins, baring his teeth. "Surprised?"

Nellin lashes out with a kick that almost catches Bennie in the head. The Brailack hacker leaps backward into an awkward back flip, deactivating his beam saber as he does. He almost sticks the landing, tipping sideways. He recovers as best he can getting his feet under him.

Wil and Maxim continue their firing, taking down two more droids, causing the second data archive to crash to the ground.

Maxim grunts, falling to his knee, a section of his armor blackened. Wil moves next to him only to take two direct hits to his midsection, forcing him to the deck next to his friend. Cynthia is by his side firing wildly, forcing the droids to duck and dodge.

Gabe moves in from behind, firing rapidly a single energy bolt into each of the droid's heads, dropping them to the ground.

Bennie and Nellin circle each other. "You could cut me down in a heartbeat. What's stopping you?" the Tygran man demands.

Bennie looks past his opponent, who has put his back to the rest of the *Ghost* crew. "I wanted my friends to be able to watch." He leaps into the air, beam saber igniting as he brings it down in a tight arc. He doesn't sever his opponent's arm from his body, but the blade cuts into Nellin's shoulder deep enough to ensure the limb is useless.

Nellin roars, kicking backward where Bennie lands, catching the hacker square in the back, driving him to the ground several meters away. The hilt of his beam saber skids to a rest a meter from its owner, deactivated. Nellin stalks towards Bennie as the Brailack is getting his feet under him. He produces a knife from a sheath on his hip. Bennie rolls to avoid the first slash but Nellin quickly back hands his opponent sending him sprawling again. He kneels on Bennie's back. "You're going to die." He raises the knife, then jerks, making a squishy gurgling sound.

Bennie looks up to see half of Nellin's neck and lower jaw burnt away. Ichor pumps from the wound as the man falls on top of Bennie.

"Hello, this is GNO News Break," Mon-El Furash says, her eyes dark, and her large fan-like ears are no longer covered in jangly earrings. "Things have escalated quickly." She breathes, looking directly into the camera pickup. The air around her is smoky, and several light fixtures seem to be out.

"I'm still aboard the *Pax Imperious*. We've engaged the mysterious ships, and the fighting has been fierce, to say the least." She looks around. "I believe the unknown vessels have retreated and the Peacekeeper force is holding off their pursuit to make repairs. Several ships were lost in the initial fighting. This new enemy possesses powerful ships and weapons."

She takes a breath. "I'll be back with an update shortly. Stay strong and keep our brave Peacekeepers in your hearts, friends."

# CHAPTER 20_

# TIME TO GO!_

"Gross! Get him off of me!" Bennie screeches. Cynthia rushes over, leaving Wil and Maxim to support each other as they hobble towards their friend.

Gabe and Jacoby join as Wil and Maxim reach Bennie.

Gabe reaches down and plucks the corpse from his friend, tossing it aside. He turns to Wil. "Good shot."

The sound of the *Ghost's* cargo doors sliding apart breaks the silence.

"I was aiming for his head," Wil admits. "That was considerably grosser than I intended."

Gabe stairs at him, unblinking, then turns to Bennie. "You acquitted yourself well."

Bennie stands with Cynthia's help. "Thanks. Guess my training isn't complete."

Maxim grunts, "You can still kick Wil's ass."

Bennie tuts, "Who can't?"

"Hey!" Wil shouts in protest. "Fuck you guys, I have other skills."

Maxim raises an eyebrow as Zephyr, Len, and Sekma walk down the *Ghost's* cargo ramp, the former saying, "We should go. I think this place is gonna explode." She continues toward Maxim, helping him up the ramp.

Gabe points to the nearest data archive. "Should we take them with us?"

As the others walk and hobble up the ramp, Wil rubs his blackened midsection. "Yeah, I think so." He looks at Jacoby. "Can you get the other?"

The hybrid man nods, his jaw clicking.

From the rear of the landing bay, someone shouts, "Hey! Don't forget about me!" Demfley flops and wiggles her way out of hiding.

Wil looks around. "Has that klaxon been going off this whole time?" Several lights in the ceiling are strobing red. An alert klaxon is bleating.

"Yes," Gabe replies. "This station is going to explode." Dropping the data archive, he turns and strides towards the large hybrid, picking her up as if she weighs nothing.

Wil looks at the ceiling, rubbing his side. "It didn't just start?" He grabs the handle on the side of the archive, dragging it behind him.

"No," his mechanical friend replies as he and Demfley approach.

"Can you tell how long we have?" Wil grunts, starting up the ramp as Jacoby passes, the data archive balanced on his shoulder. Wil watches the bigger man pass, frowning.

"Toph's tampering with the wireless network is prohibiting me from gaining any useful information." Wil opens his mouth, but Gabe continues, "However, the reactor has reached a level of instability that my sensors can detect from here. So..." he shrugs, extending an arm to hurry everyone up the ramp, balancing his passenger with ease.

"...Boom impending," Wil finishes.

"Indeed." Gabe inclines his head. He walks up the ramp, dropping one of the data archives next to the control pedestal just inside the cargo doors at the top of the ramp.

Wil follows, dropping his archive just inside the threshold of the cargo doors. He rushes toward the staircase leading up to the common deck above.

The rungs of the ladder rattle under his armored steps. "Everyone get to your stations. We gotta go!" As he rushes through the lounge area, Wil presses a control on his wristcomm. The undamaged sections of his armor click as they disengage, falling to the floor. The torso armor, with its blackened and deformed side, doesn't immediately fall away as he passes through the hatch into the "neck" of the ship connecting the large aft section to the bridge, armory, and airlocks. "Damnit." He slams a fist against the damaged section of armor, wincing. He reaches both hands into the stubborn section of armor, pulling and grunting until it falls off just outside the bridge.

Wil drops into his seat and looks around. "Jeez, what the hell?" He powers up the flight systems.

Zephyr walks in. "Sorry about the bridge."

Wil looks at her. "At least you didn't let mister thorny sit here." He looks over at Cynthia's station. "You get to tell Cyn." He powers up the repulsor lifts and the sub-light engines at the same time. The *Ghost* lurches a bit as she leaps out of the spacious cargo bay.

WIL PUSHES the sub-light throttles all the way forward, pushing the *Ghost* away from the exploding repository of criminal trinkets and trophies. He taps the intercom. "Hold onto your butts!" A second later, the blast wave catches up to the Ankarran Raptor, tilting it wildly, forcing Wil to keep a white-knuckle grip on the flight controls. The ship shakes violently, several components burn out sending sparks raining down. Alerts flash up on several consoles. The ship evens out as the wave of energy passes, dissipating as it goes.

Zephyr looks over at Wil. "You know, this will definitely not endear us with the Consortium."

He frowns, turning to look at his first officer. "Yeah, we gotta make sure they never find out. I don't want those assholes all over us again." He watches a display on his console tick off the distance between the *Ghost* and the system's bright blue star, thirty minutes to safe FTL distance. He slaps his console, engaging the auto flight system. "Remember that guy that looked like Ziggy Stardust?" He shudders.

"Oh yeah, what was his name? 'No one ever escapes me,'" she says in a mocking tone.

Wil laughs. "Good times." He turns more serious. "Think Nellin sold us out?"

Zephyr shrugs. "No way to know. Let's hope not." She grins, baring her teeth. "I know who we can ask though."

The bridge hatch opens. "Everyone is settled in. Luckily exoskeletons don't bruise," Maxim says. He looks around. "Dren." He steps inside the bridge. "This place looks like wurrin."

Zephyr makes a face. "You're welcome for removing the bodies."

Bennie shoves past the big Palorian. "Did Wil crash, and I missed it? What the wurrin happened here?"

Wil flips off the Brailack hacker. Bennie looks at his console as he gets closer. "Is that blood?" He pokes at his chair. "Gross!"

Cynthia pushes past Maxim. "Woah." She moves toward her console, looking at it in dismay. "What the..."

Zephyr rubs her face. "You know, Branx is in the brig. Maybe we get some answers?"

Wil looks at his first officer. "Don't think this means you're off the hook." He leans over to Cynthia's station and plucks a two-inch thorn from the seat. "For all this."

Zephyr's voice raises an octave. "How is this my fault? I kept them from taking over the ship with nothing but a non-verbal Sylban and a research droid that doesn't like confrontation." She pushes everyone out of the bridge. "Whatever. No respect."

The Ghost's brig is the opposite of spacious; in fact, it is downright small. The security anteroom is not much bigger. While Wil and Zephyr are in the cramped space looking at the display that shows the single cell, the rest of the crew waits in the lounge and prepares dinner.

"Hi," Wil says.

On the display, Branx opens his eyes and sits up on the lower bed of the bunk bed against the wall. He looks around until he spots the camera pickup. "Here to tie up a lose end?" he growls. Both of his large ears are bruised and drooping slightly, the cartilage in each broken.

Wil looks at Zephyr, pressing the mute button. "Damn, girl." His first officer just shrugs. He turns back to the display. "Who was your contact? Did Nellin go to the Consortium?"

The Malkorite man snorts. "Why should I tell you anything?"

Wil tuts, "Well, if you haven't gathered, you're the only one of your team left. We're on our way to Tarsis. Tell us, or don't, but you'll definitely tell your interrogator on Tarsis." He takes a breath. "Look man, I just want to know what kind of pot full of shit Nellin dumped us into."

Branx grunts. "Guess you'll find out."

# YOU TAKE THE GOOD, YOU TAKE THE BAD_

Cynthia looks up. "He give you anything?"

Wil closes the hatch to the common stairwell and says, "Nope." He looks at the kitchen counter. "What're we having?"

Zephyr moves to the lounge and drops onto the sofa next to Maxim, making Bennie bounce off the cushion. She says, "I'm guessing he doesn't know. Nellin didn't strike me as the kind of leader that shared details with his underlings."

Maxim nods. "Yeah. I never liked him."

Zephyr clucks, "Shame, he was so sexy."

Cynthia nods her agreement, purring.

Wil looks at her. "Hey."

"What? He was hot," she protests. "He was—what did you call that woman from the movie? A smoke show?"

Wil grimaces. "Whatever. He's dead, so who's sexy now?"

"Still not you," Bennie quips from the arm of the sofa. He shrieks as Maxim leans over and shoves him off the arm of the sofa to the deck.

Wil looks back to Cynthia. "Where's Gabe?"

"And what's for dinner?" Zephyr repeats.

Cynthia turns to the cooktop. "Oh, yeah, sautéed sea skippers, and Gabe is down in the hold with Len, Jacoby, and the others." She looks over her shoulder. "Go get the table set down there. Demfley can't come up here. I'll be down in a microtock."

Wil opens the hatch to the stairwell. Maxim, Zephyr, and Bennie grab dishware and utensils from the table and head through the hatch.

"Greetings, Captain," Len says as Wil descends the stairs. The research droid and Gabe look up from whatever it is they are working on.

As the crew reaches the cargo hold, Jacoby comes over. "You get anything from your prisoner?"

Wil shakes his head. "He's not being cooperative."

Jacoby's lower arms unfold, making fists. "Maybe I should give it a shot?" His mandibles spread open, revealing the serrated teeth that are normally not visible.

Wil holds up a hand. "Zephyr thinks Nellin didn't share any details with his crew. She's probably right." He pats the bug-like man on an armored shoulder. "Besides, the PKs will definitely get something out of him, if there is anything to be gotten." He grins wolfishly.

Bennie walks over to Len and Gabe. "What are you two working on?"

Gabe points to a device that looks like the grav sled he constructed for Demfley previously. "Version two."

Len dips their head. "This version should be much more comfortable for her, and adaptable."

From a few meters away, the woman that now resembles a sea turtle says, "I'm very, very excited."

Bennie examines the device. "Can I help?" The two droids nod their heads.

The hatch at the top of the stairs opens. "Dinner is on!" Cynthia shouts.

AFTER DINNER, WIL FIRES UP THE PROJECTOR. WITH FEWER occupants, the impromptu seating they had put together previously is in more ready supply.

As *The Princess Bride* begins, Jacoby leans over, the chitin of his exoskeleton creaking. "Can I speak with you?"

Wil nods, standing. They walk over to the large cargo doors. "What's up?"

"I wanted to thank you." The man that looks more like a three-meter-tall cockroach than a Multonae offers his thick armored arm.

Wil grasps the other man's arm, his eyes locking on the chitinous area where Jacoby's eyes would be. "No thanks needed."

"Nevertheless. If it hadn't been for you and your people," he inclines his head toward the two droids working on Demfley's sled, "and Len, we'd be dead. That station would have collapsed."

Wil blushes. "I'm sorry the others didn't make it."

"They died free, doing something good." The insectoid man shrugs as best his body can allow. "I'm sure they would want it that way, if they had been asked." His smile makes Wil's skin crawl. He turns to the bulkhead the movie is playing on. "You know most of us can't see the movies, right?"

Wil leans back. "I thought you all could more or less still see things. Why didn't anyone say anything?"

Jacoby points to Sekma. The thorny Sylban is sitting on the deck, hugging his knees to his chin, rocking back and forth, watching the movie. The mutated thorns that protrude from his body make scratching sounds on the deck.

Jacoby laughs. The sound is a mix of clicking and barking. On the screen, the man in black is rolling down a hill shouting, *As you wish*.

# CHAPTER 21_

# GOING HOME_



"Independent transport *Ghost,* you are cleared for landing. Welcome back to Arcadia," the space traffic controller says over the speakers in the ceiling.

Wil nods, imagining that he is speaking to a cement mixer named Stacy. "Copy that, Arcadia control." He presses a few buttons, accepting the nav plan. Ghostly green lines appear on the primary display.

The crew has spent the trip from the Consortium station to Arcadia cleaning up the ship. Sekma's thorns prove to be especially difficult to remove from upholstery.

"Ouch!" Bennie shrieks, tilting in his seat. He reaches down, and when he raises his hand, a three-inch thorn is pinched between two thin green fingers. "Did that overgrown shrub even sit here?"

Zephyr smiles. "Not that I recall, no."

Bennie turns to glare at Wil. "You put this on my seat, didn't you?"

The ship shakes as she enters the upper atmosphere. Wil doesn't look at the angry Brailack. "Busy flying, don't want to crash." The barest of smiles creeps onto his face.

"Krebnack," Bennie growls.

On the primary display, plasma streamers are flitting across the shields. In the distance, First City's massive arcologies are reaching into the clouds.

Maxim whistles. "I don't think I'll get tired of seeing that." He turns to Bennie. "You gonna hang out a bit longer?"

The Brailack makes a gagging noise. "No. This place sucks if you're a biological. I'll give them time to dial in the hospitality features first." He hitches a thumb over his shoulder towards Wil. "Plus, I want to get to work on Team Awesome Headquarters."

Zephyr looks up from her station. "I'm sorry, the what now? Team who?"

"Team Awesome," Bennie repeats. He shrugs. "We have a home base now. Shouldn't we have a name? We gotta put something over the door."

Wil's eyes dart from the display to Bennie and back again. "Not Team Awesome, that's for sure!" He adds, "You didn't have anything over your door."

Bennie clucks, "Because 'Bennie's Fake ID and Hacker for Hire Emporium' wouldn't fit."

Cynthia says, "What about Omega Force?"

"Taken," Maxim says.

On the primary display, the spaceport has grown to take up the entire screen. The *Ghost* has slowed down. Wil presses a control, and several loud clunks echo through the ship, the powerful landing gear deploying and unfolding.

"Don't crash," Bennie says.

"Fuck you," Wil replies.

"Are you sure?" Zephyr asks as Len walks past her down the cargo ramp.

The research droid turns to look at her. "I am. I am not an adventurer."

Maxim tuts, "I don't know, you just had a pretty amazing adventure."

The droid turns their head to Maxim. "Yes, and I was," the droid tilts their head, "freaked out the entire time."

From inside the cargo hold, Wil laughs. "They said 'freaked out.'" He turns back to what he's doing.

Len looks at Maxim and Zephyr. "Thank you for allowing me to earn some level of redemption for my part in their treatment."

Zephyr looks over her shoulder at Jacoby, Demfley, and Sekma. She turns to Len, nodding. "It was our pleasure."

"Okay, we gotta go!" Wil shouts from inside the cargo hold.

Len steps off the ramp as Gabe appears at the top. "Please say hello to interim Governor Mitch for me."

Len nods. "I will."

The ramp raises as the cargo doors slide shut. Maxim and Gabe turn to Jacoby and his friends, the big Palorian man asking, "You sure you want to come with us to Tarsis?"

Jacoby nods. "That cranky councilwoman promised to help us."

Wil shrugs and heads for the stairs. "Next stop, Tarsis." The sound of the cargo doors grinding shut drowns out anything else he says.

"What the wurrin?" Maxim asks as they drop out of FTL in the Tarsis planetary system. The *Ghost* is still several billion kilometers from the planet. Hundreds of Peacekeeper ships are seemingly scattered everywhere at random, covering Lagrange points and various orbits.

"Party?" Wil asks. "There are more here than last time."

He's going to continue, but Cynthia interrupts, "Woah." She looks up from her console as everyone turns to look at her. She looks back up and nods to the primary display where a window appears with the latest GNO news cast.

When the show ends and the window closes, Wil says, "What the ever-loving hell?" He looks around. "I mean seriously, more funky alien-looking ships? Did Asgar have like a failsafe plan or something?"

Maxim shakes his head. "Those weren't Farsight."

Zephyr nods. "He's right." She frowns. "This has to be Janus."

Wil makes an exaggerated sighing sound. "Man, that guy sucks." Zephyr nods.

Cynthia's console beeps. She taps a few commands, and over the bridge speakers, a bored sounding space control operator says, "Independent starship *Ghost*, you're cleared for landing in spaceport Sneldon Galp. Sending flight guidance now."

"Sending to you," Cynthia says as an indicator on Wil's console lights up.

He nods. "Got it." On the primary display, ghostly green lines appear threading their way through the congested orbits of Tarsis.

"I'm picking up another two dozen PK ships out past the fifth planet. Must be a rally point."

Cynthia says, "We're all invited to dinner."

Wil looks over his shoulder. "Yum," he says dryly.

THE LANDING PLATFORM IS FAR MORE CROWDED THAN THE LAST time they were on Tarsis. Several luxury transports are crowded into the space, as well as what look to Wil like military transports. He points at one of the latter vehicles. "Those PK?"

Maxim looks. "Yeah, personal transports for upper rank types. Wonder what's going on?"

Wil looks at his friend. "We don't want to know. We don't want to get involved." He holds up two fingers, first pointing to his own eyes, then tilts them to point at Maxim's. The big man grunts his agreement.

Gabe strides along ahead of them toward the pedestrian exit, Bennie perched on his back. Wil looks at the others. "What the hell is that?"

Cynthia shrugs. "He convinced Gabe that his legs were tired." She shakes her head.

Outside the spaceport, a luxury shuttle is waiting. Bennie and Gabe are already inside. A Tarlack woman is standing outside the shuttle. Her eyes bulge on seeing Demfley's grav sled. "What is that?" She points.

Wil looks over his shoulder. "A friend. Open the cargo hatch on that thing."

The Tarlack woman taps her front two feet impatiently, her antennae flattening against her skull. "I was not informed—" Wil waves her protest away. She frowns and taps an icon on the screen of her wristcomm. The rear of the vessel hisses as the large rear cargo hold opens.

Wil looks at Demfley. "I'm afraid it won't be as luxurious."

The woman that used to be an Olop chuckles, her beak-like mouth clicking. "I'm used to it." She drives her sled into the back of the shuttle.

Wil turns to their escort. "Now we can go." She frowns and raises an arm for the rest of the crew and surviving hybrids to enter the shuttle.

Jacoby sits down, shifting this way and that. The Tarlack escort looks over. The shuttle lifts off the ground with the slightest of vibrations. "Are you uncomfortable?" Her antennae twitch forward and back.

Jacoby's jaw clicks. "I don't bend the same way anymore." He stands up, grasping the ceiling, digging his clawed fingers into the wood inlay. Their escort frowns at the damage.

# A JOB SORTA WELL DONE_

"Captain, you were supposed to not make a *thing* out of this," Councilor Selmak says from her end of the table.

Wil and the crew of the *Ghost* are sitting at a long table in the Councilwoman's spacious office complex. It is not the same long table they sat at weeks ago when the Councilor and Barbara Mress hired them to rob the most secretive and powerful, and largely unknown, criminal organization in the Galactic Commonwealth.

Wil sets his glass down. "This is good."

Barbara Mress raises an eyebrow.

Cynthia offers, "Things went a little sideways."

"As usual." Maxim mumbles.

Bennie stands on his seat, reaching across the table to spear a piece of jerlack. "I think we did pretty well, all things considered."

Selmak tuts, "You do, do you? The surviving droid who knows the most about this research is back to being a hermit on Arcadia. The group of hybrids you found, a group of unique individuals who could have been instrumental in uncovering the secrets of this unknown DNA, are mostly dead."

"You got two," Maxim offers.

The elderly Tarsi woman fixes Maxim with a look that makes

him squirm. "If I cut off all but two of your fingers, would you at least still have two?"

"Dark," Wil mumbles. Maxim inclines his head, conceding the point.

"Not to mention, one of the data archives was damaged. Your droid friend has been working on it for two days, to no avail," Selmak adds.

Wil holds up a hand. "Hey, we didn't break it or know it was broken when we got them."

Barbara looks at her colleague waving Wil's protest aside. "What Selmak means is—"

The other woman tuts, "They know what I mean. They screwed this up."

Wil holds both hands up this time. "Hey, that's not fair. It was your team that caused the problem. Nellin and his team. Remember them, Shadow Six, your fancy fixer team? The team you foisted on us, I might add." Wil glares at the Tarsi Councilor. "He set up a deal with someone for those arcs. His team killed the other hybrids. Not us. You want to be all cranky with someone, go take it out on Branx. He's in our brig waiting for pick up." He stares until the Tarsi woman shifts in her seat.

Cynthia looks at Mress. "He's right. We got in, did the job, and were ready to go. The moment Nellin knew we had the archives, he signaled his team."

Selmak nods slowly. "As you said." She takes a bite of her salad. "Well, we have what we needed." She looks up at Mress. "None too soon."

Zephyr looks around the table. "The attacks?"

Selmak bows her head. "We believe your old friend Janus is finally making his move against the GC."

Wil swears under his breath. "We figured the same. I guess we knew it was too much to hope for that the Source baddie ate him."

Bennie looks around, placing his hands on the table. "So, how much are we talking here?"

Mress and Selmak look at each other, then turn to Bennie, the Tygran woman asking, "How much what?"

"Money, duh," the Brailack replies. "You're about to hire us to take care of Janus, right?" He holds his beam saber hilt up to show it off.

"Wait, what?" Wil asks, looking at his small green friend. He mouths, *We talked about this.*

Selmak makes a noise that must be what Tarsi sound like when laughing. "No. What in the dreams of the great maker makes you think you could accomplish something like that?" She waves Bennie away. "That's a pretty toy. Perhaps if you had ten thousand of them, you'd be useful." The Brailack frowns.

Wil turns from glaring at Bennie to the surly old Tarsi woman. "Wait just one second." He puts a hand on his chest. "We've saved the GC, what?" He turns to Maxim. "Three?" The big man inclines his head. "At least three times."

Selmak grunts, "Yes, well we'd prefer to leave the saving the GC to the professionals." She smiles. "With a little help from the data archives you recovered."

Cynthia raises a hand. "I'm sorry, how are those arcs going to help?"

Mress answers, "Our hope is that the archives, and the hybrids, can help us find," she looks around, "something to defeat Janus and this Source creature. We assumed we had more time."

"You knew about Janus and the Source," Maxim says.

Selmak looks at Bennie, then Maxim. "Well, duh. For one thing, you made a full report to Jark Asgar. We have all of his records." She smirks. "For another, while I understand you have an outsized opinion of your abilities, this invasion force could rival the Peacekeeper fleet. Such things get noticed."

"What? How is that possible?" Maxim asks, leaning forward. "When we saw Janus' fleet, it was at best a large task force."

Selmak sighs, looking at Mress. "How these people saved anything is beyond me."

Mress smiles. "You just need to get to know them." She turns to the others. "According to our intelligence sources, while it's taken Janus time to make his move against the GC, he's been busy in the outlying regions, well away from our reach."

"And eyes, in some cases," Selmak adds.

Mress takes a breath, adding, "He's been building and stealing ships this whole time."

"Well, this all sounds terrible." Wil stands up. "You don't want or need us, so..."

"Pay the balance due," Bennie adds, then yelps as Zephyr smacks him on the back of the head.

Wil rubs his face. "Unless there's anything else?"

Selmak nods, tapping the PADD in front of her, causing Wil's wristcomm to vibrate. She looks up. "If there is anything else you can share about Janus, or more importantly, this Source creature he's allied with..."

Wil nods. "We'll share what we know, but most of it was in our report to Asgar." He adds, "Don't forget to send someone for Branx."

Mress walks over to them. "She may not see your value, but I do. Keep in touch." She rests a hand on Wil's shoulder, then hugs Cynthia. She nods to the others. "Be safe out there."

Wil nods. "Always are."

# CATCHING UP_

"You guys get your thing done?" James asks.

Wil grunts, "Yeah, more or less." The *Ghost* is on its way back to Fury. Jacoby and the hybrids saw them off after everyone checked out their new living quarters in a scientific tower on Tarsis. Selmak assured the crew of the *Ghost* that they'd be well taken care of.

"Get paid?"

"Of course," Wil says. He looks at a small window set in the display. "Gotta make this quick. We're almost home."

"Why do you guys always go to Fury?" James rubs his chin. "You told me it was a shit hole."

Wil grins. "It very much is, but it's a shit hole we know. It's as close to a safe harbor as anywhere else." He shrugs. "Plus, we've gotten to know the place. It's comfortable."

His friend raises an eyebrow. "Why don't you just set up a base or something then? Don't you live on the ship when you're there?"

Wil laughs. "You got a bug on the ship? We actually just closed on a place before this little adventure started."

"On Fury?"

Wil shrugs. "Like I said, shit hole we know. Plus, there's this place. Think of a TGI Friday's, but you know, in space, like on Tatooine or something. The fried zerglings are amazing." He thinks a second. "And there's a burger—well it's ground jerlack, which is like a cow but has enormous eyes and these cute little wings, really tasty. Oh man, gonna have to stop there when we land." He grins. "Anyway, the food's good and the real estate is cheap. Well, cheaper than most other planets." He shrugs.

His friend sighs. "Seems like a solid reason to establish a base." He smiles. "Always thinking with your stomach." He gets serious. "What're you gonna call yourselves?"

"What do you mean?"

James grins. "You got a building, gotta put a name on it." He snaps his fingers. "Space Team!"

"Taken, I'm pretty sure." Wil grins. He snaps his fingers. "Oh! Another plus for Fury: only a token Peacekeeper presence." He grins. "And even less government."

"There we go." James points at the camera pickup, grinning.

Wil leans forward. "So, how're things there?"

James' pointing finger turns into a flat palm he wiggles up and down. "So so. Earth First looks like they're going to get some seats on the Alliance Council."

"That sounds bad," Wil says.

"It's not great, but they won't have a majority, so we'll see how well they play with others," James replies, then adds, "By the way, thanks for that ship ID database."

"You find your friends?"

"Sorta. Both look like modified versions of Zamxin Skimmers. Know anyone that uses them?" James says after consulting something off screen.

"Only most of the criminals in the GC," Wil says. "It's a popular model. Bigger than a Raptor by two or three times, but slow. Well armored and easy to mount guns on." He locks eyes with his friend. "Light a fire under someone's ass. You should beef up your planetary defenses. If someone is sniffing around, they're thinking of paying you a visit."

James nods once. "Lovely."

Wil looks at a small window set in the corner of the display. "I better go."

"What about A-Team?" James presses. His brown eyes are twinkling with glee over the name.

"Dude, taken, probably copy-written." Wil resists.

"What, like they could sue you in space?"

"Space lawyers, dude. They're out there." Wil grins.

James nods. "I'll keep working on it. I'm glad we get to talk more now. Take care, man."

Wil smiles. "Likewise, and you, too."

WIL EXITS HIS QUARTERS AND RUNS RIGHT INTO GABE, knocking himself to the deck. Gabe reaches down, offering his hand. "Sorry, Captain."

Wil stands up, brushing himself off. He looks up at his mechanical friend. "There a reason you were lurking outside my quarters?"

"Lurking has such a negative connotation," the droid replies. Then he adds, "Yes, there is a reason. I wanted to apologize for the damage to the archive."

Wil smiles at his friend. "Nothing to apologize for. There was no way you would know about those safe guards ahead of time." He pushes his friend toward the stairwell down to the common deck.

Falling in behind his Captain, Gabe says, "Indeed. Nonetheless, one archive was rendered irrecoverable."

Inside the stairwell, Wil stops and turns to his friend. "If the GC can't figure something out, and we have it, we'll make sure they get it. Making a copy was a CYA for us." He looks around. "But listen, this is between us. No one needs to know we have that data. Lock it away deep, double and triple encrypted."

"That is not a thing."

Wil makes a face. "You know what I mean." Gabe puts a finger to his mouth, running it across like a zipper. Wil laughs and continues to the common deck, opening the hatch and seeing the rest of the crew. "Who's ready for some home renovations?"

## THE END

# EPILOGUE_

WIL WALKS into the room he and Cynthia claimed as their own in the warehouse that is now the team's permanent home on Fury. "I've got it."

Cynthia looks up from what she's reading on a PADD, "Is it contagious?"

Wil makes a face. "Hardy har har." He drops down next to her on the bed. "I know where we should go on vacation."

She sits up. "Ok, where?"

He grins. "You'll see."

"I thought we'd settled on Arcadia?"

He shrugs. "Better idea. Especially after hearing about Bennie's adventure."

ACKNOWLEDGMENTS_

Thank Beta/ARC team

Chris Boyd
Alice Clark
Steve Rakoczy
Việt Thanh
Meenaz Lodhi

## THANK YOU_

Thank you so much for reading Space Rogues 8: Here, There Be Monsters

**If you enjoyed it I'd love it if you left a review. Seriously, reviews are a big deal. They help readers find authors. They help authors show how awesome they are. :)**

Reviews are social proof and go a long way to encouraging other readers to take a chance on an unknown.

# OFFER_

As they say, there's no harm in asking, so here we go.

If you can help connect me with someone who can get Space Rogues on a screen (Big or Little) I'll cut you in for 10% (Up to $10,000) of whatever advance is paid.

Send me an email and we can discuss.
rights@johnwilker.com

# STAY CONNECTED_

**Want to stay up to date on the happenings in the Galactic Commonwealth?**
Sign up for my newsletter at
johnwilker.com/newsletter
Lots of goodies await you, just sayin'

Visit me online at
johnwilker.com


If you like supporting things you love by sporting merch, well you're in luck! I've launched a Space Rogues Shop, take a look.